The First Time Ever Published!

The First Ghost Cat Cozy Mystery

A Brand New Mystery Series from New York Times
Bestselling Author

Jessica Beck

GHOST CAT: MIDNIGHT PAWS

D1132492

To Sim, absolutely the greatest cat I've ever known!

Ghost Cat: Midnight Paws Copyright © 2013 Jessica Beck

Chapter 1

As I stood in the hallway on a dark autumn afternoon searching the bookshelves for something to take my mind off my crushing sadness and pain, I felt the unmistakable brush of a cat's tail caress my leg, a sensation that any cat lover in the world would recognize. Before I could look down, though, a sudden movement above caught my eye, and I spotted my Russian Blue cat, Shadow, sitting on the top of a bookcase halfway down the hall.

An icy chill raced through me the second I saw him watching me from so far away.

The reason? I had only one cat now.

It had been three days since my Black Bombay cat Midnight's life had been extinguished by the same robber who'd killed my boss, Cora Anthony, and there was a hole in my heart so big from the double loss that I doubted it would *ever* go away. If I hadn't had Shadow to lean on lately, to stroke endlessly, to whisper my pain to, I don't know if I would have made it. It was bad enough losing my employer and dear friend, Cora, in such a senseless act, but while I'd cared for her, if I was being totally honest about it, Midnight had meant even more to me.

So much so that apparently I was still feeling phantom brushes from his tail against my leg.

When I looked down and saw Midnight's ghostly image sitting on the floor below me, I nearly fainted on the spot.

"Merw?" he asked plaintively in his softest voice, the one that always told me he was worried about me. For folks who didn't understand cat language, it probably sounded a great deal like any other comment Midnight might have made, but I knew my cats so well that I could read every inflection in the sounds they made. All I had to do was hear a single comment from either one of them, and I knew precisely what was on their minds.

I shook my head, trying to clear the cobwebs away. I was clearly seeing *and* hearing things now. I'd been in mourning for the past three days, and I doubted that I'd had more than a random bite of toast or a half-hearted sip of water in all of that time, something definitely out of the ordinary for me. I enjoyed eating, and I usually wasn't ashamed of who knew it.

"You're just overwrought, Christy," I said softly to myself. "It's perfectly reasonable that you'd be imagining all sorts of things right now." I closed my eyes, counted to ten, and then I told myself that no matter how much I wished it might be otherwise, Midnight was gone.

When I looked back down at the floor, I was relieved— and yet also more than a little saddened—by my late cat's absence.

Maybe it was time I got something a little more nourishing to eat before I started seeing my parents again too, though they'd both been dead for years.

I was walking into the kitchen when I happened to glance up at Shadow, searching for some reassurance that I still at least had one cat in my life.

That's when I stopped dead in my tracks.

There on the ledge beside Shadow was the faint presence of Midnight, looking down at me with an expression that told me that he knew something that I didn't.

Clearly, that was a fact that I was in no position to dispute.

I was still trying to come to grips with what I'd just seen when the telephone rang.

"Hey, Christy, it's me. How are you holding up?" It was great to hear Marybeth Jackson's voice. She was the best friend I'd ever had, and her call was exactly what I needed after what I'd just seen. We'd been roommates in college at UNC-Asheville, and now we were living together again in her grandparents' former house in Noble Point, North Carolina, located snuggly in the Blue Ridge Mountains. It was a creaky old place, with sloping floors and not a square right angle in the entire building, but it suited both of us perfectly.

"I'm hanging in there," I said. I would have loved to tell her what I'd just seen, but Marybeth was skeptical of all things supernatural, and I knew for a fact that she didn't believe in ghosts of any kind, whether they sported two legs or four.

"Have you had anything to eat today?" she asked.

"Gosh, Mom, I don't remember," I said with the hint of a smile, despite the heaviness in my heart. The moniker was what we always called each other when one of us was being overly solicitous toward the other.

"I'm going to take the high road and ignore that, if that's okay with you. What do you think about me taking off work early so we can hang out together?" she asked.

I knew how important her career was to her as a pharmaceutical company's drug rep, so it was no small sacrifice on her part to make the offer. "As much as I appreciate the gesture, you don't have to do that. I'm okay."

"Sure you are. And just think, with me there, you'll be even better. I'll see you in a few hours, Roomie."

"Thanks, Marybeth."

"You bet."

After we got off the phone, I grabbed a cinnamon-raisin bagel from the counter and then went off in search of Midnight. If I was truly losing my mind and seeing things, it probably wouldn't be a good idea to tell anyone else about it, but I still had to see if my ghost cat was still around.

"Midnight. Shadow. Come here." No response, and both cats were gone from their perches above the bookshelves.

"I've got treats."

The offer was my last resort, one that I always had to follow through with or take the risk that neither one of them would ever come back to me again when I called them.

Unfortunately, I didn't know what kind of treat a ghost cat would like, but it ultimately didn't matter.

Neither one of the rascals came to me when I made the offer. It was a big house, though, and I was still looking for my wayward cats when I heard the front doorbell ring. As I walked from the back parlor through the hallway toward the front of the house, I glanced up and saw that Shadow and Midnight were both back on top of the same bookcase where I'd found them earlier.

If Shadow was at all surprised by his roommate's sudden reappearance from beyond the grave, he wasn't showing it.

"Neither one of you go anywhere. I'll be right back," I ordered, not at all sure that they would listen to me, no matter what side of the grave they might be on.

I opened the front door and said, "Oh, it's just you," as I realized that Lincoln Hayes was standing outside on the broad porch of our house.

"I have to say, I've had warmer welcomes in my life," Lincoln said cheerfully. He was a handsome young attorney two years older than Marybeth and me, with dark brown eyes and matching auburn hair. Lincoln and Marybeth had dated off and on in high school, but they'd shifted into Full Friend mode since she'd moved back home to Noble Point. Marybeth thought that Lincoln might have developed a little crush on me since I'd moved to town, but if it were true, I hadn't seen any signs of it. Not that I was even sure that I wanted anything more than friendship from him. My heart had been broken six months before by a man with a ready smile and a treacherous heart, and I was in no mood to take a chance of it happening again anytime soon.

"Sorry, Lincoln. I didn't mean anything by that. I guess I'm just a little distracted at the moment."

"Don't give it another thought. It's completely understandable. Christy, I'm truly sorry for your loss." I could see the depth of his pain for me in his eyes, and it really touched me.

"Come on in," I said.

"Thanks. I overestimated the temperature when I decided

to walk over to get a little exercise. It's a little chilly out today, isn't it? I'm already starting to miss summer."

"Not me. Fall and Winter are my favorite times of year." I had a sudden notion. This was the perfect opportunity to see if I was delusional, or if my cat had truly come back to me from beyond the grave.

As Lincoln stepped inside, I said, "Do me a favor, would you? Shadow is on top of the bookcase. Come into the hallway and take a look at him for me, would you?"

As he followed me into the hallway, Lincoln asked, "Do you want me to get him down from there for you?"

I laughed at the very thought of it. "No, he's perfectly capable of getting down on his own when he's good and ready."

"Then why exactly am I looking at him?"

"Just indulge me, okay?"

Lincoln frowned a little, and then he nodded. I had to know if Midnight was really there, or if he'd just made an appearance in my grief-stricken imagination.

Lincoln stepped into the hallway, and I held my breath.

"Is that supposed to be funny?" Lincoln asked a moment later.

"What are you talking about?"

"He's not there," Lincoln answered.

"Are you sure?"

"See for yourself."

I glanced through the hall past him and saw that my cats were indeed both gone from their earlier spots. I couldn't blame Shadow for taking off if he'd decided that he didn't want to share his place with Midnight. He had every right to freak out even more than I did by his companion's sudden mysterious reappearance, though he hadn't shown it so far.

"Should I look for him?" Lincoln asked.

I knew my cats better than that. If either one of them wanted to vanish, they were perfectly capable of disappearing without the slightest bit of effort, ghostly state or not.

"Never mind," I said. I'd deal with them later. "What brings you by?"

"Christy, we need to talk," Lincoln said gravely.

"That's what I thought we were doing."

That didn't even merit a smile. "This is serious. I'm sorry, but it really can't wait any longer. I've tried to give you as much time as I could. Why don't we go back into the living room and have a seat?"

The living room was in the front section of the house, not to be confused with the back parlor. Marybeth had spent a great deal of time here during her summer vacations as a kid, and when her grandparents had moved to Florida, they'd deeded the house to her as an outright gift. I was happy to be a renter, coming to Noble Point to visit my best friend three months earlier and surprising us both by staying, even finding a part-time job at Memories and Dreams, Cora Anthony's eclectic shop filled with odds and ends and curiosities galore. At the time, it had seemed like the perfect place for me to figure out what I wanted to do with my life.

At least that was how it had stuck me until three days ago.

"How about if we go into the kitchen, instead?" I suggested. "I can make us some coffee. You look like you could use a cup."

The young attorney smiled gratefully, and from the developing bags under his eyes, I could see that he had indeed been working too hard lately. "Actually, that sounds great."

We went into the kitchen, and I saw unsurprisingly that our main coffee pot was nearly empty, and undoubtedly cold. Marybeth and I loved our coffee, and it wasn't all that unusual for us to have two pots brewing at the same time, creating magical elixirs from the far regions of the globe.

"I'll put a fresh pot on. Don't worry; it won't take long," I said as I rinsed out the remnants of our last batch in the sink.

"Don't go to any trouble on my account," he said.

"I'm not," I said, adding a brief grin. "It sounds good to me, too."

"Okay, that's perfect, then. While we're waiting for the coffee, we can go ahead and get started." Lincoln opened his briefcase, really just a fancy men's messenger bag, on the kitchen table and pulled out a sheaf of papers.

As the attorney pushed them toward me, he said, "I need you to sign everywhere there's a yellow arrow. I've marked everything for you to make this process easier. Your full name is Christine Olivia Blake, is that correct?"

I pushed the documents right back at him without replying.

"What's wrong?" he asked.

"Besides the fact that I have no idea what you're asking me to sign, everything's just peachy."

"Didn't anyone tell you?" he asked, looking haggard.

I shook my head. "I don't really know how to answer that, do I? If they'd told me, I'd know, but if they didn't, would I have any idea what I was missing?"

"I don't understand. Someone from my office was supposed to call you yesterday to let you know what was going on," he said.

"Well, they didn't."

Lincoln frowned slightly. "I apologize for that. I would have called you myself, but I've been buried in paperwork lately."

I must have flinched at the word 'buried,' because he quickly added, "Poor choice of words. Things have been crazy around the office. Sorry."

I tapped the documents. "Are you going to tell me what's in there?"

He tried to smile, and he nearly made it as he announced, "What it all boils down to is that you've been appointed as the acting manager and caretaker of Memories and Dreams."

"What are you talking about?"

"She didn't tell you? Cora changed her will two weeks ago. She wanted to give the whole business to you outright, free and clear, but if she did that, she knew her two greedy cousins would challenge the will in court if she cut them out completely."

"They can have every last bit of it as far as I'm concerned," I said. I had no interest in running the place, or ever taking one step through that front door again, whether it was on Cora's terms, or any others. A part of me had died in that shop right alongside Midnight, and I *never* wanted to go back.

"Don't be hasty, Christy. It would mean a substantial pay raise immediately," Lincoln said, "and a controlling ownership interest in the business as well after a set trial period. It's nothing to throw away without some serious consideration first."

"Lincoln, I don't *have* to take it, do I?"

"Don't you want to stay in Noble Point?" he asked softly. For the first time, I could see that Marybeth's teasing about Lincoln's crush on me had at least some basis in reality.

"I don't know. I haven't really thought that far ahead yet."

"I know for a fact that there are a lot of folks in Noble Point who would like you to stay, including me, but if you've already made up your mind, there's still time to figure out how you'd like to handle this. In the meantime, while you're considering your next move, you should take this offer," Lincoln said.

"Why?"

"I can give you a dozen reasons why it makes sense, but there's really only one that matters. It's what Cora wanted," he said softly.

"So you say."

"You don't have to believe me. It's all right here in black and white."

I glanced over at his messenger bag. "You don't happen to have a letter or anything from her in there explaining all this to me, do you?" It didn't make sense. Cora loved writing cryptic puzzles and rhymes for me, and then leaving clues that helped me solve them. Why hadn't she done it now, when it was most important?

"What are you hoping for, Christy, a message from beyond the grave? I'm afraid there's nothing." Lincoln frowned for a second, and then he added, "I do know that she wanted you to do this. She was pretty insistent on it, as a matter of fact."

Lincoln flipped through the documents, and then he pointed to one of the pages in back that was headed with the word 'Codicils' on it.

I glanced at it, and then I pushed the papers back at him again.

"Don't you believe what I'm telling you is true?" Lincoln asked.

"That's not it. I can read all of this for myself, but that still doesn't mean that I'll understand it. If you want me to have a clue about what you're talking about, you're going to have to do better than that."

He picked up the top document, and then he read the pertinent information aloud.

"Sorry, but it still doesn't make sense to me. I didn't go to law school, remember?"

Lincoln nodded as he studied the document again. "Basically, it says here that after two years of operating the shop as its general manager, you inherit fifty one percent of the company, with the option of buying out the other two owners at the fair market value of the business. If you choose not to buy them out, they have the option of buying your share from you, but not until those two years have passed."

"Do they get the same percentage breakdown that I do?" I asked, curious about the odd terms of the agreement.

Lincoln frowned. "Not quite. They only have to pay *you* half the market value to buy out your share if they want you out."

"There's got to be a mistake there," I said.

"No, Cora was most emphatic about how she wanted the

document worded."

"How would you know that? Did you draw the will up yourself?"

"I may have consulted with her about it," he said, clearly hedging a little.

"Come on, spill. What was her rationale behind this oddball arrangement? Did she give you any idea what was on her mind?"

"I probably shouldn't say anything, but it was Cora's wish that you take over the shop in her absence. The salary is such that if you watch your money and don't get too carried away with your spending, you'll be able to afford to buy your partners out without too much difficulty. Cora had me set the document up so that the value of the business on paper will decrease over the next two years, while its actual value should grow. The arrangement will help you if you buy it outright, but in the same light, it will cost you a fair amount of cash if you decide to sell out. It was the best way she could think of to get you to stay."

"Is that it, then? Have my other two partners signed it yet?"

"Hang on a second; there's more that you don't know yet. While it is true they have lesser stakes in the business, they are not allowed on the premises while you are in charge. If either one of them come within one hundred yards of the shop, they automatically lose their share of the inheritance."

I had to laugh. "Cora wasn't a big fan of theirs, was she?"

"Evidently she owed their mother a rather large favor—that's the only reason they're in the will at all—but I gathered that she wasn't fond of either one of them. You know Cora, though. She always said, 'Debts are paid. No excuses.'"

"I know. I certainly heard it enough myself. At least no one will be looking over my shoulder if I decide to take over, which I'm not. Is there anything else I need to know?"

"You may choose two items in the shop, regardless of

their market value, for yourself. That applies whether you take the deal or not."

That caught me off guard. "You're kidding, right?"

"Lawyers don't kid, at least not about things like this. I'm supposed to go with you, record what you take, and then have you sign these papers." He glanced at me, and then added, "Or refuse them. It's your choice. Are you ready to go?"

I had just had a ghost cat show up suddenly in my life, and I still had to do a world of grieving. The last thing I wanted to do was to return to the scene of the crime where I'd lost so much.

"I can't do it, Lincoln," I said, choking out the words through my sudden tears. "I don't think I'll ever be able to go back there."

"I suppose that makes sense,"   the attorney said sadly. "I'm just sorry that you're going to miss out on this opportunity, not that anybody with a heart could blame you. I'll take a rain check on that coffee, if you don't mind."

We stood, and as I led him back into the living room, I felt that brush against my bare leg again.

Still expecting Shadow, I was startled to see that it was Midnight again.

"Do you see that?" I asked Lincoln as I stared down at my ghost cat.

"See what?" he asked as he looked intently at my leg. "What happened? Did something bite you?"

Midnight shook his head in contempt, whether with me or the lawyer I couldn't say, and I felt a chuckle die in my throat. Evidently, I was the *only* one who could see him.

For a split second, I'd forgotten that he was gone.

After he looked back at me one last time, Midnight did the most startling thing I'd seen, if I discounted his reappearance a few minutes earlier.

He walked through the front door as if it weren't there, and I raced to open it after him.

I had to see where the rascal was going, though I had a

sneaking suspicion that I already knew.

Chapter 2

"Where are you going?" Lincoln asked as he raced to catch up with me.

"I need some fresh air," I said. "Would you care to join me?"

"If we're not going to the shop, I'm sorry, but I've got a mountain of paperwork to do back at the office," Lincoln said.

If my suspicion was correct—and knowing Midnight, it was going to be on the money—I needed Lincoln to get me in the front door of that shop, since Cora had been very protective of who had a key.

"I changed my mind. We're going to Memories and Dreams, but I have to do it on foot. Come on, it's not that far, and it's not that chilly out, either." Sure enough, we were heading down the sidewalk toward Cora's shop. Midnight was leading me back to a place I didn't want to go, but there had to be a reason for it. Was he trying to tell me that he needed me to see where he'd ultimately lost the battle of his life, no matter how valiantly he'd fought? Or was there some deeper and darker purpose to the visit? Was there something there that had to be done, a wrong corrected, before he could move on to a happier place? And did I fit into his grand scheme somehow?

No matter what the reason, I had no choice. As much as I hated the idea of going back into the shop, I couldn't stand the thought that I might be letting down one of the best friends I ever had as he was making his last request of me.

The three of us got to the sidewalk in front of the building, and I saw that the police tape had been removed from the front door. If it bothered Midnight to be back there at the scene of his demise, he didn't show it. He simply walked through the closed door of the shop, and without thinking it through, I reached for the doorknob and tried to follow him.

"Hang on. I've got the new key in here somewhere." The locks were changed earlier, according to Cora's wishes."

Lincoln was still fumbling around for the key when Midnight's head popped through the door, looking for all the world like a trophy mounted on a wall. He gave me his best 'impatient' expression, and then he added a 'mew' that questioned my basic intelligence and my ability to understand and obey simple instructions.

"Take a chill pill, will you?" I said with a hint of aggravation in my voice.

Lincoln asked, "What are you talking about? I'm not upset about anything."

"I wasn't talking to you," I said. Somehow it had just slipped out before the filter in my brain had a chance to stop it.

The lawyer stopped his quest for the key as he looked around. "Nobody else is around here, though."

"The key, Counselor. Focus."

He nodded, trying to hide the confusion I could see on his face, but I didn't know what else to say that wouldn't make it worse, so for a change of pace, I decided to keep my mouth shut.

Midnight watched us a few seconds longer, and then he must have grown bored with the proceedings. I saw his head duck back through the solid door, and I couldn't wait to see what was so important on the other side.

Lincoln found the key at last, and turned it in the new lock.

As the door opened, I walked inside, scanning the room as I searched for Midnight.

Of course, he was nowhere in sight.

Lincoln glanced at his watch. "Do you have any idea what you might like to have for yourself? You get two choices, so I'd make them count, if I were you."

"I'm not sure," I said, pretending to study a few pieces as I searched for my cat. A sudden thought struck me, one that iced my veins. Was that why Midnight had come back from the Great Beyond, just to lead me to Memories and Dreams? Would I never see my old friend again now that I was where he wanted me to be?

"Merwerw." I heard him scolding me before I saw him. He was batting away at an old wooden box, his paw going straight through it, nevertheless doing his best to draw my attention to it. I picked the box up, but it looked like a thousand other odd things Cora had collected over the years. I flipped it open and saw that the interior was lined with faded red velvet. Resting inside was a faded letter, but it was difficult to read. Was that what Midnight was trying to tell me? I started to tuck the letter into my pocket when Lincoln asked from just behind me, "That's what you're picking? Are you serious? I think you're wasting one of your choices, Christy."

I had no choice but to slip the letter back inside the box, and then hand it to him. "This is what I want."

"I don't get it," Lincoln said as he studied the markings on the box.

"You wouldn't understand. It has sentimental value," I said, trying to come up with some reason for my seemingly irrational act.

"Fine, but I wouldn't worry about emotions on your next pick. I understand that there are a few really valuable items here," he said as he pointed toward our selection of antique furniture.

"They aren't worth as much as you might think," I said with a smile.

"What do you mean?"

"Quite a few of Cora's antiques aren't all that old. She has a man in Asheville who makes knockoffs for her."

"Cora cheated her customers?" Lincoln looked quite surprised by the revelation. "I knew she liked to gossip, but I never dreamed that she misrepresented her offerings here."

"Take it easy. Cora always told them what they were buying before she'd sell any of it. She prided herself on her integrity, and she would never do anything to jeopardize that.

Cora figured that if her clients knew exactly what they were buying, what they did after that was their problem and not hers."

"There's got to be something else here you'd like," Lincoln said. "What about a nice piece of jewelry?"

I looked around to see if Midnight was going to give me another hint about what to take, but he was gone.

I just hoped that it wasn't for good.

Suddenly, I knew just what I wanted. I headed for the jewelry case and picked out a gold pendant that I'd had my eye on for months. It was the thickness of two quarters glued together, the rough size and shape of a domino, and to make it even better, a large "C" was engraved on its face. If I could have afforded it, I would have owned it the second I'd first seen it.

"This is what I want," I said.

Lincoln nodded. "That looks like a fine choice." He pulled the documents out of his bag, filled in a few blank areas, and then he had me sign where he indicated.

"Is there any chance that you've changed your mind about taking Cora's deal?" he asked as I put the necklace around my neck.

"As a matter of fact, I have," I said, clearly startling him by my sudden reversal. I figured that Midnight might not be done with the shop, and if I gave up my right to be there, I wouldn't be able to follow his next lead.

"When can I get started?" I asked.

Lincoln glanced at his watch. "I believe it can wait until tomorrow for you to open back up to the public. In the meantime, here are both copies of your new key."

The attorney handed them to me, and then he said, "If there's anything I can do, and I mean anything, please let me know. You have a great many fans here; you know that, don't you?"

"That's nice of you to say."

He wasn't about to accept that, though. "Christy, I mean it. Don't underestimate the power of your friends."

"Thanks," I said as I started to follow him out of the shop.

"Aren't you staying behind to check on things inside?"

"No, I think I've done enough for one day, don't you?"

"Absolutely," he said.

After I locked the door behind us, he asked, "Can I walk you home?"

"Lincoln, your office is right down the street. It's not on your way, and we both know it."

"I don't mind. I have time for a little detour," Lincoln said.

"Don't worry about me. I'll be fine."

I said good-bye, and then I raced back toward the house. Was Midnight there waiting for me, or was he gone forever? All I knew was that I couldn't wait to find out.

Chapter 3

"There you are," I heard Marybeth say as I walked back into the house we shared. By her own admission, my best friend was twenty-five pounds over her ideal weight. That being said, she also had wavy blonde hair and big blue eyes that made men fall madly in love with her at first sight, something I'd seen happen more than once myself. "I was about to call 911."

"I was with Lincoln," I said. "He came by the house, and then we went out." As I spoke, I jammed the wooden box from Cora's store deep into my pocket. I never would have chosen it myself, but Midnight had been so insistent that I hadn't really had any choice. I'd had to force myself to hold off examining it again until I had some privacy, and now it appeared that I had a little longer to wait than I'd thought.

"Well, well," she said with the hint of a smile. "What was he doing, giving you some grief counseling?"

"*Really*, Marybeth? Do you think that's the least bit appropriate, given what's happened lately?"

"I don't know. I understand that a lot of people deal with grief by turning to someone close to them," she said.

"You know me better than anybody in the world. Does it sound like something I might do in your wildest dreams?" I asked.

"No, of course not. I'm sorry; you know that I didn't mean anything by it." Marybeth took a deep breath, and then she asked, "If Lincoln wasn't here to console you, then why were you together? I'm sure he didn't come by to see me."

"You never know. He might have been wanting to stoke up an old flame."

"Trust me, that's not even an issue. I've seen the way he looks at you," she said with a knowing smile.

"How exactly is that?"

"Like a dog staring at a porterhouse steak," Marybeth

said.

I shook my head and laughed at the imagery. "You're too much. You know that, don't you?"

"Girl, you have no idea. So, if the barrister wasn't here for romance, why *was* he here, and where did you go afterwards?"

"He had some papers for me to sign," I admitted.

"Regarding?"

I *really* didn't want to get into Cora's will if I didn't have to. "I could tell you that it's none of your business, but it wouldn't do me any good, would it?"

She laughed. "I suppose that you could try, but we both know that you'd just be wasting your breath."

Marybeth was right. I decided then and there that my best course of action was a direct admission of everything—with the exception of Midnight's reappearance—or I'd never get her off my back. "Cora left me the majority share of her business, with a few pretty big provisos."

"That's wonderful," Marybeth said as she started to hug me. When I didn't reciprocate, she pulled back. "What's wrong?"

"Honestly, I'm not sure I can ever get over what happened at the shop."

"But you're still going to do it, aren't you? You have to at least *try*, Christy."

I studied her for a few seconds before I spoke. "Marybeth, you seem awfully eager to have me stay."

"What can I say? I've grown accustomed to your constant snoring and your unpredictable hygiene habits."

Since both those charges were grossly unfounded, I chose to ignore them. "You're just afraid that you won't be able to find anyone else who's willing to live with you in this big old rambling house, aren't you?" I asked.

"Guilty as charged," she said with a grin. "What should we do this evening? A celebration is probably out of order."

"By a dozen degrees," I said. "I'm going to take things day by day, and just do my best to get through them, at least at first."

"That sounds like a good plan to me. In the meantime, I'm hungry. Are you ever going to get your appetite back?"

"As a matter of fact, I think I have," I said, startled by my own admission. It could have been that part of my grief had run its course, but more likely, it was directly due to Midnight's reappearance in my life. I knew that having his ghost around wasn't going to be anywhere nearly as satisfying as having him with me when he was alive, but his presence meant a great deal to me, and if this was the only way I could have him now, then I was going to embrace it. Midnight might be gone for the rest of the world, but for me, he was still there, still an important part of my life.

"Excellent," Marybeth said as she rubbed her hands together. "Should we start with some weak broth, since it's been so long since you've had any solid food?"

"I was thinking more along the lines of a loaded pizza," I said. I wasn't sure how much of it I could eat, but I had to at least start trying.

"Even better. I'll grab a menu and my phone, and then I'll call our order in."

As Marybeth left the room to retrieve the take-out pizza menu, I quickly pulled out the box that had been burning a hole in my pocket. I cracked it open, not sure what I might find there.

To my surprise, it wasn't a letter at all.

It was a poem, written in Cora's sloppy handwriting.

The riches of the world are hidden away,
Masked in the Devil's light.
A chest of fire burns deep within,
Hiding the heart of Midnight.

Was that why the daft cat had been signaling for me to choose the box? Did he somehow recognize his name? Had I honestly just wasted one of my inheritances on a bad poem and a plain old battered wooden box? Or was this the final puzzle Cora had left me?

"Midnight," I said with a hard edge in my voice.

"*Really?* Are you *kidding* me?"

My ghost cat chose that moment to poke his head through the closed front door and walk into the house. He spied the poem in my hand, looked at me with self-satisfied smugness for a few seconds, and then he turned and went back out the way he'd come in. Was it my imagination, or had he lingered as his nether regions passed through the door, giving me his opinion of my intellect and intuitive skills?

"Cats," I said in frustration just as Marybeth came back into the room.

She looked around for a moment, and then asked, "Christy, who are you talking to?"

"Thin air, apparently," I said as the tip of Midnight's tail vanished. That cat had a lot of nerve, criticizing my reasoning skills when he himself appeared to be as mad as a hatter. To be fair, he had acted no different before his ghostly transformation.

"Okayyyy," she said, stretching out the last letter of the word for emphasis. "The pizza will be here in half an hour. What should we do in the meantime?"

I tried to put the poem away, but my roommate was too quick for me. I managed to hide the box back in my pocket, though, but it was a marginal victory at best.

Before I could stop her, Marybeth snatched the paper out of my hands. She read it quickly, and then she handed it back to me. "*You* didn't write this, did you?"

"No, Cora did," I said.

Marybeth frowned at it another second, and then she added, "It's not very good, is it?"

"I don't know. It has its merits," I said.

"If you say so. As for me, I'm more of a Robert Frost kind of gal myself."

"To each her own," I said, folding the paper back up and sliding it into the same pocket that contained the box. There had to be more to its significance than Midnight's name, but I had no idea what it might be.

"So, what should we do while we're waiting for our

food?" Marybeth asked. Apparently she was willing to cut me a little slack, given my state of mind.

"Do we have any ice cream?" I asked.

"Now you're talking," my roommate said with a grin. "I'll get the gallon in the freezer and a couple of spoons."

"Sounds good to me," I said. "I'll meet you out on the porch."

I walked outside, fully expecting to see Midnight lolling about in the sun, but he was nowhere to be found. Wherever he'd gone, I knew it was pointless to search for him. Midnight—or any cat, really—had a mind of his own. When he was ready to show up, he would, and not a minute before.

I watched from the front porch as the world passed me by, no one really noticing me, each person intent on reaching his own destination. Even though Noble Point was a small town, enough of the distractions of the world still seemed to seep in from around the edges to occupy the vast majority of people's attention. That was one of the reasons I loved my cats so much. They kept me in the here and now, grounded in the things that mattered: food, shelter, companionship, and love.

I was just beginning to feel sorry for myself when I felt the weight of a feather settle onto my lap. Like a Cheshire cat, Midnight had chosen to materialize, touching me, and I could swear I felt the whisper of him before he'd appeared. My cat had changed when he'd become a ghost, but the essence of him was still there, with every swish of his tail and every mew he uttered. He was changed beyond the boundaries of science and faith, but for whatever reason, his essence was still with me. Midnight was gone, but in a very real sense, he'd never left me. My fingers stroked his back casually, almost without thought, and for an instant, he was there with me in all his glory.

When the door opened and Marybeth came out carrying our first course of ice cream, Midnight vanished as though he'd been nothing more than a stray ember from a campfire hitting a lake's rippling surface.

"Sorry. Am I interrupting something?" Marybeth asked.

"No, I was just thinking about Midnight," I confessed. Well, it was true, in its own way, and the world, if nothing else, was full of gray areas, now more than ever.

With my ghost cat now gone, Marybeth and I sat side by side on the porch swing, our spoons dipping into the carton of chocolate ice cream in a choreographed dance that complemented our motions perfectly. I felt more reassured by Midnight's brief presence than I had any right to. His choice to be with me made all the difference, and if there was anything I could do to ease his transition into the next world, I would. Midnight deserved justice, and if it was within my power to help him achieve it, nothing short of the very ends of the earth would stop me.

Marybeth took a heaping spoonful of ice cream, dispatched it quickly, and then she said, "I can't put my finger on it, Christy, but there's something different about you."

"I don't know what it could be," I said. "I haven't done anything new since the last time you saw me."

She studied me. "Is it the hair? No, that's still the same sad style you had in college. The clothes? I don't think so. Hey, that's what's new. I like the 'C,'" she said as she touched my necklace lightly. That was one of the reasons that I'd been first attracted to it, and Cora had admitted that it had drawn her in as well from the first second that she'd laid eyes on it. "It's nice. When did you get that?"

"I guess you could say that it was part of my inheritance. Cora's will let me choose two things to have for myself, and this was one of my picks."

"It's beautiful," she said. "What else did you get?"

I wasn't eager to show her the faded wooden box I'd chosen, even if I never planned to tell her the reason for its selection.

"I chose a wooden piece," I said.

"Where is it? Is it inside, or are you having it delivered? I hope it's a new coffee table. I hate ours."

"It's nothing that big," I said.

"Is it another necklace?"

"No, it's not jewelry," I said.

"Then what did you get?"

There was no way I wanted to pull out my sad little box. "It's nothing, really."

"Then why did you pick it? Come on, Christy, now I'm just getting more and more intrigued, and you know how relentless I can be once I get my teeth into something."

"Trust me, I know that better than anyone else."

She smiled at me brightly, clearly not offended by my agreement in any way. "So, what did you choose?"

I knew I wasn't going to get away with hiding it from her, so I reached into my pocket and pulled out the wooden box I'd chosen based on Midnight's reaction to it.

Marybeth took it from me, turned it over a few times in her hand, opened it, closed it, and then she gave it back to me. "What made you choose that?"

"My ghost cat asked me to," I felt like saying for a moment, but I knew that I couldn't utter those words. I'd given Lincoln a simple, though false, explanation, so I decided I might as well stick with it. "It has sentimental value to me," I said.

"The only thing I'm sentimental about is money," Marybeth said, though I knew for a fact that she was lying. She still had every birthday card she'd ever received tucked safely away in a box in the attic, and other boxes were there as well, each labeled, 'Marybeth's Memories.' I'd stored one of my boxes along with hers, which she'd quickly marked, 'Christy's Junk'.

Sometimes treasure, like beauty, is in the eye of the beholder.

"Well, it's not worth anything in that respect," I said as I took it back. As I reached for it, I must have knocked it out of her hands by accident. It slipped through both sets of our fingers and landed hard on the tiled floor. There was a sharp wooden crack as it hit the tough surface below.

"I'm so sorry," Marybeth said as she reached for it.
"It was my fault," I said as I beat her to it. Without even
looking at it, I shoved it back into my jacket pocket.

Marybeth was about to pursue her relentless
questioning—I could see it in her gaze—but something
stopped her. It would have taken a nuclear meltdown to
divert her attention away from me, but thankfully it was
nothing that drastic.

Happy Times Pizza pulled up, and I knew that food
would distract my friend more than anything I could say or
do.

We were just finishing our meal when a blue and white
police cruiser pulled up in front of our house. Sheriff Adam
Kent, a heavyset older gentleman who fancied himself a
ladies man, was the law in Bluemont County, and he also
happened to be Marybeth's uncle.

As he got out of the squad car, he hitched up his belt, a
constant tugging motion that had worn part of the beige
leather of his belt to brown.

"Ladies," he said as he tipped an imaginary cap in our
direction.

"Would you like a slice of pizza, Uncle Adam?"
Marybeth asked. "There's plenty left." I'd had trouble
eating more than one piece, though Marybeth had done her
part.

He looked into the box, and then asked, "Are you sure
you're both finished?"

"We're done," I said. The sheriff had been the one to
deliver the bad news to me about what had happened at the
shop on my rare day off three days earlier during a raging
thunderstorm. Cora had complained about being lonely
whenever I wasn't there, and on a whim, I had offered her
Midnight for company. How I longed for that decision to
make over again.

Sheriff Kent nodded, retrieved a napkin, and then
devoured the remains of the pizza in the box with startling

enthusiasm. "Excuse me; I haven't had time to eat today."

"I'm just sorry there's not more," Marybeth said.

"I could surely use a soda to wash it down," he said.

"I'll get it," I said as I started to get up.

"I'd rather Marybeth do it," he said.

"Why, is there a certain way you like your drink that I don't know about?"

Marybeth said, "He wants to talk to you alone, Christy. I don't mind."

"Is that true?" I asked.

"It is for a fact. This little girl here knows me too well."

"You're not all that hard to read," Marybeth said as she retrieved the empty box and the paper plates we'd eaten on. "Just call me when you're finished chatting."

After she was gone, Sheriff Kent said, "You're lucky to have her as a friend. She's a fine young lady."

"I'd like to think that we both are," I said, not meaning to let my voice sound snappish. There was a certain breed of Southern gentleman who didn't believe that women should lift heavy things or think deep thoughts. Their mere presence made the hackles on the back of my neck stand up. I didn't know the sheriff well enough yet to say whether he was that kind of fellow, but it was beginning to look like a possibility.

"I'm sure you are. I came by to update you about what we've uncovered about the homicide."

"That should be plural, shouldn't it?"

He looked at me steadily to see if I was serious, and when I didn't back down, he nodded. "Yes, ma'am. You're right. My apologies. I'm sorry to say that we aren't having much luck tracking the killer down. Do you happen to know if Cora kept an inventory of her goods on hand? If something was stolen from her shop, we can try to catch the killer when he tries to fence whatever he took."

"Sorry, but there was nothing ever formally written down about what we carried. Cora somehow kept it all in her head."

The sheriff's chin sank a little with the news. "That's too

bad."

"It's not completely hopeless, Sheriff. I might be able to help."

He looked startled by the suggestion. "How could you do that? You haven't worked there all that long, have you?"

"Several months, actually. As a matter of fact, I'm managing the place now," I said, "and I've always paid attention. I know just about everything we have that has any real value."

He touched his chin as he said, "That's an interesting way to put it, Christy."

"Why do you say that?"

The sheriff looked at me for a full second before he spoke again. "All in all, you came out of this in pretty good shape, didn't you?"

"Except for losing my *cat*, you mean? Trust me, I cared more about him than anyone or anything else on the planet, whether you think that's strange or not. Midnight was more than just my cat. You might not understand it, but he was my best friend, too." I suddenly realized that I was crying, but only after I tasted the saltiness of my tears as they hit my mouth.

Marybeth exploded out onto the porch. "Uncle Adam, what did you say to her?" she asked as she wrapped me up in her arms.

"I didn't say anything," he said, clearly befuddled by this turn of events.

"He thinks I had something to do with what happened at the shop," I said through my tears.

"He *doesn't*," Marybeth said fiercely as she let me go. "He *couldn't*." She looked at him harshly for a moment, and then she asked him directly, "Do you?"

"Marybeth, I can't eliminate a suspect just because she happens to be a friend of yours," he said. "There are questions, no matter how uncomfortable they might be, that have to be asked."

"Get off my porch," she commanded.

"Don't push it, child. I spanked your bottom when you needed it as a youngster, and don't think I won't do it now."

"That's funny. I remember taking a chunk out of your finger the last time you tried to spank me," she said. "Care to see if I can bite all the way through this time?"

The sheriff backed off the porch, clearly surprised by his niece's reaction. "This doesn't concern you, Marybeth."

"When you come here accusing my best friend of having something to do with murder it does."

The sheriff laughed harshly. "*You* might think that the two of you are close, but she just told me that *cat* of hers was her best friend."

"Of course he was," Marybeth said. "You know I've never been a big cat fan, but Shadow and Midnight are different."

"What, like people?" He clearly thought we'd both lost our minds.

"In a very real way, they are better than we are," I said.

"I give up," the sheriff said in frustration. "We'll finish this later."

"I don't think so. I'm done talking to you," I said.

"You might think so, but then again, you'd be wrong. Draw up an inventory of anything that's missing and send it over to me ASAP."

He reached to shake my hand, and I didn't want to take it at first, but manners in the South are bred from birth, and it was a hard habit to break. As I took his hand, he held onto mine and pointed to my locket with his free hand. "Is that something that should go on the list? It looks valuable."

"It was a gift from Cora," Marybeth said.

"I'm sure it was," he said, not even attempting to hide his disbelief.

"Ask Lincoln Hayes," I said. "It was in her will."

"I'll do that," the sheriff said as he let go of my hand.

After he'd driven away, Marybeth said, "I'm so sorry. I don't know why he's acting that way."

"I didn't help matters. I overreacted," I admitted. "He

just wants to find the person responsible for all of this."

"Doesn't he realize that you do, too? You've got more at stake here than just a job. This is personal."

"You bet it is," I said, suddenly spent from the confrontation with Sheriff Kent. He'd been well within his rights to question me, and I shouldn't have fallen apart like I had, but there was a great deal more anger and rage inside me than I'd realized. Something told me that if there was going to be justice for Midnight, I was going to have to take matters into my hands.

I had an edge on the sheriff, though.

I had a cat who could walk through walls and see behind closed doors.

If only I could figure out a way to get him to tell me what he knew.

Then again, maybe that was exactly what he was trying to do.

Chapter 4

"Get off me," I said groggily in protest as I came out of a deep sleep to find a cat nestled on my chest. I thought I'd broken Midnight and Shadow of their desire to sleep on top of me a long time ago.

"I'm serious," I said as I tried to brush the offender away. I'd been having the nicest dream, filled with memories of two living, though sometimes cantankerous, cats. It had felt so real, so natural, that I never wanted to wake up.

Until a set of claws dug into me.

I half-expected to find Midnight there, but it was Shadow, and he was clearly upset about something. I tried rubbing his head between his ears—a spot that was guaranteed to settle him down most days—but not even that was doing any good at the moment.

"What is it? Is something wrong?" I asked plaintively, wishing for the thousandth time that he could actually answer me.

"Would you like something to eat?" I asked him. I was wide awake now, and I stared over at the alarm clock beside me bed.

It was 4:20, and the night outside was as dark as Midnight's coat.

"Come on," I said as I reached for my robe, still holding onto Shadow. So far he'd shown remarkable aplomb dealing with his lost colleague, but I knew that it could easily just be a matter of time before he showed his loss more overtly. Having Midnight's ghost return was disturbing to me on a great many levels. How on earth could Shadow handle it without having at least a little bit of a meltdown himself? If sleeping on my chest helped him to get a little peace, I was just going to have to start wearing three layers of sweatshirts to bed.

Downstairs, I checked his water bowl, and saw that it was

nearly full. He clearly wasn't thirsty.

"How about a snack?" I asked. In some ways, having a cat and a baby were remarkably similar. Like a small child, a cat couldn't convey the reason for its unease, and it was sometimes a matter of guessing until the right answer appeared.

Shadow had no interest in a snack for the second time that day, an event that was becoming more and more disturbing to me. In the echoes of the moonlight coming in through the kitchen window, it was clear how my pawed friend had gotten his name. He seemed to come in and out of focus as clouds raced across the sky, showing the moonlight for a moment, and then hiding it again.

"What is it?" I asked him. "How can I help?"

Shadow sniffed the air twice, sneezed once, and then curled up on the countertop and promptly fell fast asleep.

Cats.

I started back to bed when the clouds vanished and Midnight suddenly appeared at my feet.

"Mewrwer," he said, as if he had been expecting me all along. I suddenly realized that Midnight hadn't appeared on the second level of our house since he'd shown back up as a ghost. Was there something about his spectral state that kept him close to the ground? He clearly wasn't afraid of heights, in this life or the next. Hadn't I seen him on the bookcase with Shadow earlier?

Shadow.

It suddenly all made sense. When he'd realized that Midnight needed me, he'd woken me up and then he'd lured me downstairs. Only then, once his job was accomplished, had he fallen fast asleep again.

"What is it? What's going on?"

Midnight headed for the living room, and I followed. Shadow would be just fine right where he was.

Midnight made it to the front door before I could say, "Hang on one second, Mister, I'm not going outside."

He paused and looked at me questioningly, as if to ask

why the delay.

"If you think I'm going to parade down Main Street in the middle of the night in my robe and my slippers, you've lost your feline mind. Whatever is so urgent is still going to have to wait until I get dressed."

"Phhht," he said, clearly showing his disapproval for the delay.

I didn't wait for any more of an answer than that. I raced upstairs, got dressed in jeans and a T-shirt as quickly as I could, and then I slipped on my Converse tennis shoes before I headed back downstairs. As I left my room, I grabbed my wallet and my keys as I threw on my jacket, unsure where my ghostly cat was taking me this time.

"I should have at least brought my flashlight with me," I said as I followed my ghost cat down the sidewalk. The day had been chilly enough, but at this time of morning, it was downright frigid. We were clearly heading back to Memories and Dreams, though I had no earthly idea why.

"Midnight, is there *any* chance that we could both get into my car and I could just drive us to the shop?" I asked him, knowing how crazy the idea would have been even had he still been alive. My cats hated riding in a car, any car, and they would fight to the bitter end to avoid it if at all possible. Our yearly trips to the vet had always been experiences that should have involved hazard pay for me, and heavy sedation for them.

As expected, Midnight didn't believe that my suggestion merited any comment.

We were close to the shop when I noticed something odd inside.

There was a light moving around among the aisles.

Someone was inside Memories and Dreams.

I reached into my pocket for my cell phone when I suddenly realized that it was still on my dresser at home.

What could I do to stop whoever was inside? I could always scream, but I doubted anyone would be able to hear me. I could probably run for help, but by the time I got back, it would most likely be too late to do any good.

There was a long line of cars parked for the night on the street, and I had a sudden thought. Rocking each one in turn, I quickly set off every alarm along Main Street.

Whoever was inside had to have heard the racket I was making, and I braced myself for a confrontation as soon as they ran outside.

I was still waiting out in front, even after the light inside the shop vanished, when the police came, sirens blaring and lights flashing.

Of course.

Leading the way was my old pal, Sheriff Adam Kent.

He stopped his patrol car right in front of me, and for a split second, I worried about Midnight darting in front of him. That particular concern was long past now, but I still couldn't help feeling overprotective towards my cat, ghost or no ghost.

The car security systems were still blaring when Sheriff Kent got out of his car, and over the sound of the alarms, he yelled, "Christy, I'm trying to cut you some slack given what you've gone through lately, but have you flat out lost your mind?"

"Someone broke into my shop," I said.

He looked at me with an arched eyebrow, and then the sheriff motioned to one of his men.

As he approached, the chief asked, "Do you have the keys?"

I reached into my pocket and pulled out the new key Lincoln had given me the day before. "This will get you in the front door."

The sheriff took the key from me and gave it to one of his men. "Take somebody with you and go check it out."

The officer did as he was told, with one of the other patrolmen following close behind.

"This is too much," the sheriff said as the alarms started to die, one by one. They were either shut off by their owners from their windows above the street, or the timers on the alarms simply ran out.

"I'm sorry, but I didn't know what else to do," I explained lamely as I kept watching the storefront.

"You could try calling me on the phone next time," he suggested.

"I would have done it this time, but I didn't think to bring it with me."

"What were you doing out here in the first place? It's a little late for a stroll around town, and you aren't exactly wearing jogging clothes."

"I couldn't sleep," I said simply. It was true, I suppose, in its own way. One of the most skilled ways of telling the truth was to confess only part of it. My own favorite method of lying was to tell the truth so unconvincingly that nobody believed me, but I wasn't about to push it by admitting to the sheriff that my ghost cat had led me there.

The officers came out a few minutes later, sparing me any need to further dig myself into a hole.

"Whoever was in there before is long gone now," one of them said as he handed me back my key.

"So, someone was actually inside earlier?" Sheriff Kent looked surprised to learn that the break-in hadn't just been in my imagination.

"They kicked in the back door and came in through that way," the patrolman admitted. He turned to me and added, "We put some plywood over the opening, so it should be okay for tonight, but I'd have someone look at it first thing in the morning if I were you."

"Thank you," I said.

The deputy nodded, and the sheriff said, "Go on, then. It's time for your patrols."

They left as quickly as they'd come, albeit without lights and sirens this time.

The sheriff stood with me in the street, clearly wanting to say something. All I wanted to do was get out of the cold and go inside the shop so I could see if anything valuable had been taken. It had to have been a real treasure to tempt a thief. Something else occurred to me. What if it had been the murderer returning to the scene of the crime? What could have lured him back, given what the stakes would be if he was caught there?

If it *had* been the killer, I only wished that I knew what he'd been after. At least I took some comfort in the fact that I might have run him off before he found whatever it was that he'd been looking for.

"Listen, I wanted to apologize about being a little on edge with you earlier today," Sheriff Kent finally said, his voice barely above a whisper. "I didn't mean to upset you, or Marybeth, either. That wasn't the real me at all. I'm sorry."

How could I hold a grudge against him after he said that? "I understand, Sheriff. You must be under a lot of pressure, and in the end, you were just trying to do your job," I said.

"True, but I could have been a lot more diplomatic about it," he admitted. "We're not used to the level of trouble we've been having around here lately. I'm getting some heat from the city council to bring in the state police, and it's been wearing on me. Honestly, I'm a pretty good guy once you get to know me."

"Why haven't you asked anyone else for help?" I asked, realizing as I said it how it must have sounded to him.

He ran a hand through his hair as he said, "If I do that, I don't have a chance of winning the next election. I've run on a campaign promise that I'm the man for the job. If I have to go running to Asheville or Charlotte or even Raleigh for help, where does that leave me?"

"It's okay to need a hand every now and then," I said.

"Not everyone around here thinks so. Would you like a ride back to the house?"

"No, thanks. I'm going inside the shop to see how bad it is."

"I'm hoping it's not too rough in there. I'm willing to wager you scared him off before he could do much damage." The sheriff actually smiled as he added, "I've got to hand it to you. That trick with the car alarms was some pretty quick thinking."

"What can I say? Sometimes you have to use what you've got," I said.

The sheriff nodded, and then he drove away, leaving me standing there in the middle of Main Street looking around for a ghost cat that clearly wasn't there.

There was only one place he could be, but I suddenly wasn't all that interested in going inside the shop to find him.

I walked over to the door, put my hand on the knob, and then slowly turned it.

Whether I liked it or not, I was going to have to get used to being back inside Memories and Dreams.

"Midnight," I called out as I walked through the door. Having his presence near me would make what I had to do next a little easier, but of course, he was nowhere to be found. Had he served his purpose in warning me of the intruder in the shop? What forces guided him now? In almost every way, his actions and behavior were exactly as they'd been before, but it was almost as though he'd gained something in crossing over the line to the other side, an awareness of his surroundings that exceeded what he'd been capable of in the past.

Another thought came into my mind, unbidden and unwelcome.

Where exactly did he go when he disappeared?

All of a sudden, I realized that I didn't want to think about that.

I turned on every light in the place after deadbolting the door behind me, but there was still something eerie about the antique linen dresses hanging in a row and the naked mannequins lined up like soldiers against one wall. Their stark appearances made them even creepier than if they'd been dressed, and I promised myself that the first thing I would do would be to fully clothe each and every one of them, no matter how that might look to passersby.

I was going to have to do something to make the place less creepy if I was going to get any work done at all. I spotted the old jukebox in the corner under some tattered blankets, and realized that some music was in order to calm my nerves. Pulling everything off the top of the jukebox, I plugged it in, praying that it would play.

I punched B-14, and the Glenn Miller Orchestra suddenly began to play. As "Moonlight Serenade" filled the night air, I suddenly felt more at ease in my surroundings, despite everything that had happened there.

I began to calm down as I tidied up the shop where the intruder had been, restoring the place to its former orderly chaos. Cora had been able to lay her hands on anything at a moment's notice, and while I was nowhere near that proficient yet, I hadn't lied to the sheriff. I had a good, working knowledge of Memories and Dreams, and before long, I was going to know it all myself.

I walked past the jewelry cases, expecting to see them ransacked as well, but I was surprised to see that they were all undisturbed. How had the intruder missed some of the shop's most valuable possessions? The pieces we offered were small, easy to carry, and they couldn't be that hard to sell on the open market. And yet every single piece of jewelry—with the exception of what I'd taken for myself—was exactly where it had been before.

How odd.

As I kept working, I found myself moving between the jukebox and the shop's need for straightening. Whoever had owned the old music maker had an affinity for Big Band music, a trait that I shared.

By the time morning's first light peeked through into the windows, I had the place fit and ready for business. Taking an old piece of cardboard, I made a NOT FOR SALE sign and propped it on the jukebox. My silent partners might not have approved of the move, but they really weren't in any position to complain, not if they followed the rules Cora had outlined for them.

As I'd worked, I'd tried to figure out exactly what the thief had been after, but in the end, I was no closer to discovering it than when I'd started. I was surprised when I'd made my inventory list of valuables to realize that nothing of any consequence was gone.

Was I missing something, or had the robberies both been completely unsuccessful? At least that would explain the return visit I'd just had.

I looked around the room for the thousandth time, trying to figure out what it could be that was so valuable that it was worth taking two lives for. One thing I *hadn't* spotted in my search had been Cora's famous notebook. For the longest time, no one knew exactly *what* she jotted down in her black and white composition book, but I'd peeked into it once when she'd stepped away from the shop, and I had been startled to find the most scurrilous gossip about folks from town that I could have imagined. I wanted to ask her about it a dozen times, but it was a difficult subject to bring up, since I'd been snooping where I shouldn't have been when I'd spotted the notebook.

I gave up for the moment, suddenly glad that I'd taken Cora's deal. I'd have plenty of time to figure it out, as long as I could keep the thief from breaking in again. The first thing I was going to do after having the back door fixed was to get a more sophisticated alarm system. The installer might think it strange that I'd spend good money guarding what some folks thought of as junk, but something inside clearly held real value to someone.

I reached into my pocket for my new key so I could lock up when I realized that on my way over here, I'd grabbed the same jacket I'd worn the day before. Still inside was the box I'd chosen at Midnight's request, but there was something odd about it when I touched it.

The box was broken from the earlier drop, split in two in a place where there had been no seam before, and as I gently pried the two pieces apart, I saw that there was a folded scrap of newspaper inside, dated the week before.

In block letters, written with a heavy hand, it said,
THIS IS YOUR LAST CHANCE.

What was *that* supposed to mean? Had it been written to
Cora? I realized from the moment I'd seen it that *she* hadn't
been its author. I knew Cora's block lettering on sight, and
this most emphatically was not it. What did it mean, though?
What was it Cora's last chance at? Was she supposed to do
something the author wanted her to do? There just wasn't
enough information, but one thing was certain: it was a
threat, clear and simple.

The only problem was that I didn't have the slightest hint
of an idea what it might be about. I tucked the newspaper
back where I'd found it and fit the pieces back together at
well. I could see the seam clearly now, but from an ordinary
glance, I doubted that anyone else would be able to tell that
the box had a secret compartment, now breached.

Chapter 5

For now, though, I had more pressing matters at hand. I was starving.

But there was something else I needed to do before I ate. If Marybeth found out what had happened from someone else before I had the chance to tell her myself, I would never hear the end of it. Despite the time of morning, I decided I had to at least *try* to give her a call.

I just hoped that she was out of bed.

"Did I wake you?" I asked Marybeth when she finally picked up on the eighth ring.

"No, as a matter of fact, I was just on my way out the door. Where are you, by the way? I've got to be in Boone first thing this morning, and on my way past your door a little earlier, I saw that you were already gone."

"Somebody broke into the shop this morning," I said, declining to mention how I'd found out about it in the first place. It was something I didn't want to get into with her, especially so early in the morning.

"That's terrible. Why didn't you wake me up? I would have come with you."

I was about to answer when I saw Kelly Madigan bang on the front door of Memories and Dreams. "Aren't you open yet?"

I pointed to the sign, and then said, "Sorry."

"Don't worry about it. I'll be back later," she said as Marybeth asked me over the phone, "What are you sorry about?"

"I wasn't talking to you. A customer wanted to get into the shop."

"You didn't unlock your door for them, did you?"

"Not until I've had something to eat first. Anyway, the reason I didn't knock on your door this morning is that I didn't see any point in *both* of us losing sleep," I said.

"As much as I appreciate the gesture, the next time something like this happens, wake me up, okay?"

"I sincerely hope that it never comes up again," I said. "I was going to invite you to join me for breakfast, but if you're heading to Boone, you don't have time, do you?"

"Sadly, no, but I will take a rain check. Where are you going to eat?"

"I thought I'd just pop in next door to the shop. Some of Celeste's French toast sounds wonderful to me about now. I really am getting my appetite back."

There was a long pause on the other end of the line, and then Marybeth said, "Maybe I could be late for my first appointment."

I laughed. "Then again, maybe you'd better hit the road. It isn't like we won't have countless other opportunities to have breakfast together."

"I know, but I can almost taste her pancakes just talking to you."

"I said that I'm having French toast," I said.

"Even better. At least have a bite for me, would you?"

"I'll have two," I said. "I'll see you this evening."

"See you then. And thanks again for letting me know what happened."

"You're very welcome."

If Celeste's restaurant had been located thirty miles away, I still would have been willing to drive that far to eat her food. She offered a variety of home-cooked meals that reminded me of my grandmother's cooking, though Celeste was less than five years older than I was. The fact that her place was right next door to the shop just made it that much more special for me.

The café's warmth swept over me the second I walked in. The painted concrete floor was dark blue this year, but with New Year's coming up in a few months, I wondered what color Celeste would go with. Every year she changed the color, and it stayed that way all year, with one exception. I didn't live in town that year, but I heard that she'd chosen a deep crimson that turned out like dried blood. She tolerated it for two months, but then she changed it to sky blue, a color that showed dirt, but had the advantage of not making the place look like a crime scene. Red vinyl-clad booths lined the walls, covered tables filled the space in the middle of the floor, and a long counter ran across the back, a barrier between the dining room and the kitchen.

"I was sorry to hear about what happened next door last night," Celeste Montgomery said as she offered a sympathetic smile. I was sure that Celeste had been a real beauty when she'd been younger, and there were still many hints in her porcelain white skin and her luxurious black hair, but working at the diner had added too many pounds over too many years, and she was more than just pleasantly plump these days.

"How did you find out so quickly?" I asked as I took my jacket off and found a seat at the bar. A dozen folks were eating there, mostly spread out in ones and twos.

"It's a small town. Folks talk," she said with a wave. "Do you need a menu, or do you know what you want?"

"Coffee, and an order of French toast, please," I said.

"Would you like any sides with that?"

I briefly considered the thick-cut bacon Celeste served, but I decided quickly that the toast would be enough. "No, thanks."

"Young lady, you're going to waste away if you don't start eating more," Celeste said.

"Nobody could ever accuse me of that," I said, though it wasn't true just now. Normally I had a healthy appetite, but with Midnight gone, I just didn't have the heart. In fact, this breakfast was a real step forward for me. Celeste's French toast was the first thing that had sounded good to eat since I'd lost my cat, though I'd enjoyed the pizza Marybeth and I had shared last night well enough. I wasn't sure that "lost" was the precise word I should use, since he'd turned back up as a ghost. Temporarily misplaced, maybe?

Celeste disappeared into the kitchen and I was sipping my coffee when Jim Hicks approached. There was a bandage on his face, so the first thing I asked him was, "What happened to you?"

"I hit my face on a tree branch I was cutting after the big storm we had the other day," the local real estate agent said as he rubbed the spot tenderly. "It was my favorite tree, but lightning must have hit it or something. At least I'll get some good firewood out of it. By the way, I've been meaning to come by. I'm sorry for your loss," Jim said. He was a tall, thin man, almost gaunt, and every time I saw him, I thought that he'd missed his calling as an undertaker. Instead, he was into real estate. He'd been after Cora to sell her business to him recently, but she'd steadfastly refused.

"Thanks for your thoughts," I said, taking another sip.

"What's going to happen to the place now? Do you know?"

"Actually, I'm going to run it myself," I said, startling myself to hear me saying it aloud. I figured that maybe if I said it long enough and loud enough, I might just get used to the idea.

Jim looked surprised to hear the news. "Seriously? That's an awfully big task for someone so young. Do Cora's cousins know about your plans?"

So, Jim was even better connected than I'd thought. "Do you happen to know them yourself?"

"Not personally," he said. "To be honest with you, I was counting on them being willing to sell it to me."

"They might, but they don't have a say in it. Cora left it to me. Why are you so interested, anyway?"

"Just between you and me, I'm getting a little tired of real estate," he admitted quietly. "I've been frugal and saved some money along the way, and I think running a shop like yours could be fun. Christy, surely you don't want to be saddled with so much responsibility running that shop from day to day. I can't imagine the profit margins are such that you can live in any kind of style. On the other hand, if you accept my offer, I can pay you enough to allow you to find your true calling at your own leisure."

"Jim Hicks, why are you bothering Christy?" Celeste asked as she walked out of the kitchen carrying my French toast. "Leave the poor girl alone."

"We were just having a friendly chat," he said.

Celeste looked at me, and I just shrugged. Seeing that, she turned to Jim and said, "Guess what? You're finished. Now, do you want to go back to your own breakfast, or are you done eating already?"

"Keep what I said in mind," Jim said with a smile as he slipped a business card under my plate. I'd suddenly lost my appetite. It hadn't taken the vultures long to start circling.

"I've changed my mind about breakfast," I said as I pushed the plate away. "Don't worry, I'll pay for it, but I just don't have the stomach to eat anymore."

"Ignore him," Celeste said softly. "Jim can't help the way he is. It's his nature. Christy, try at least one bite before you write the meal off."

I took a whiff of the French toast and smelled the loveliness of it, with cinnamon wafting in the air, and the slightest hint of the egg batter and the raisin toast. It had been fried to a golden and brown hue, and there was a small carafe nearby with real syrup in it. My mind was finished with it, but evidently my stomach had other ideas entirely as it rumbled gently. "I don't suppose it would hurt to take one bite," I said as I added the syrup and cut off a bite with my fork. An explosion of flavor went off in my mouth as I tried it, and I savored the taste and texture of the bite. This was levels above any other French toast I'd ever had in my life, including the kind my mother used to make on special occasions. "It's absolutely incredible," I said.

Celeste beamed. "Then eat up."

I decided it would be too much trouble to get it to go after all, and besides, I wasn't in the mood to eat in the shop. "Okay."

I saw her walk over to Jim's table, and after a brief conversation, he nodded, paid his bill, and left. As Celeste walked past my spot at the bar, I said, "You didn't have to run him off on my account."

"No harm, Christy. Jim just needs a reminder now and then that my diner is not a place of business for him. Besides, it feels good to give a scolding every now and then. I suppose he was pressuring you to sell the shop, wasn't he?"

I nodded as I took another bite. "He said he'd like to own the place himself. Truthfully though, I couldn't do it even if I wanted to. I'm supposed to run the shop for two years and see how I like it. It's certainly nothing I ever pushed for, but Cora was pretty emphatic about it in her will."

Celeste looked surprised. "I hadn't realized that Cora had planned things out so thoroughly." She looked around her place, and then she added, "I don't know what will happen to this place once I'm gone. Frankly, I've never thought about it. What made her plan for the future, do you know?"

"Maybe she had a premonition about what was about to happen to her," I said softly.

"There are more things at work in our world than we could ever know. Those who live on the surface lead a shallow existence indeed." I hadn't ever really thought of Celeste as being someone who believed in omens or premonitions. Then again, I hadn't classified myself that way either before Midnight's ghost had showed up the day before.

"May I ask you something personal, Celeste? Do you believe in ghosts?" I asked as nonchalantly as I could.

"Of course I do. Don't you?" Celeste asked.

"I didn't used to, but I'm beginning to believe," I said.

She looked at me sharply. "Has Cora's spirit paid you a visit at the shop?"

"No, it's nothing like that," I said, suddenly sorry I'd asked her opinion about the spirit world. I decided that at least for now, I'd drop the subject. I slid a ten dollar bill under my plate, and then stood. "Thanks for breakfast."

"You're welcome," Celeste said as she grabbed the ten and handed it back to me. "I never had a chance to offer my condolences before, so let me get this one."

"As much as I appreciate the gesture, the truth is that Cora and I weren't really all that close," I said in mild protest.

"You misunderstood. My sympathies are for what happened to Midnight."

"That's different," I said. "Thank you."

"You're most welcome. What a comfort Shadow must be to you now."

"He is," I said. Celeste's sympathy for my loss of Midnight touched me, and suddenly I needed to get out of there before I started crying. "I'll see you later," I said.

Some of the folks eating noticed that I was crying, but I didn't care. I needed to get out of there before I broke down completely, and I didn't care what anyone thought. All I wanted to do was get in the shop before I ran into anyone else.

No such luck with that, though.

Kelly Madigan was standing there waiting for me in front of Memories and Dreams.

I looked at my watch. "I still have forty-five minutes until I'm supposed to open the shop, Kelly," I said.

"This won't take a second," she answered, and then her voice faltered. I found it odd that she was staring at my shirt.

"What's wrong?"

"That necklace. Where did you get it?" she asked.

I'd nearly forgotten that I was still wearing the second pick I got from Cora's shop. I tucked it back into my shirt as I explained, "It was a gift from Cora." While that might not be technically true, the spirit of it was.

"I was going to pick that up the day of the robbery," Kelly said. "It's mine."

I frowned as I zipped my jacket up. "I'm sorry, but it's not for sale. I'd be more than happy to help you find something else," I said.

"I'm not interested in anything else," Kelly said.

"Come again," I called out after her as she stormed off down the sidewalk. I was afraid that I hadn't won any points for customer relations, but I was keeping the necklace for myself. After all, the wooden box Midnight had chosen wasn't exactly something I cared to have for my own. The cryptic poem and newspaper-printed note had raised more questions than they'd answered.

At least the necklace was a simple and uncomplicated parting gift.

Or so I thought.

Brushing Kelly out of my mind, I unlocked the door and started getting ready to open the shop on my own. We offered a wide variety of things for sale, from antiques to jewelry to clothing to the oddest collection of odds and ends anyone in this small town had ever seen. We were three steps above a flea market or a yard sale, but not quite up to the elegant antique places I'd seen on my trip to Ireland after graduation. It had been a gift I'd promised myself, and I'd used a nice-sized chunk of what was left from my inheritance from my parents to do it. I hadn't regretted a single dollar or euro, I'd spent. The money might be gone now, but the memories I'd made would last a lifetime, and really, what better bargain was there?

As I walked in and locked the door behind me, I realized that I hadn't done anything about fixing that back door. At least I knew exactly who to call. Cora always used Emily Nance for the ongoing jobs she needed done around the shop, and I'd grown to like her from the start.

"Hey, Emily. It's Christy from MAD." That was what we called the shop in shorthand, at least we had until Cora's abrupt passing. Several other folks were in on the acronym as well, including Emily.

"I heard you had a visitor this morning," Emily said.

"Let me guess. You need me to come by and fix your back door first thing."

"Have you been eating at Celeste's?" I asked her.

"No, why, does she have a new Special?"

"Not that I know of. If you weren't there, how did you hear about the break-in?"

"I ran into the sheriff, and he told me all about it," she said. "We were both at the drugstore over in Landslide." The nearby town—named, reasonably enough, for the many landslides that often seemed to hit it—was twenty minutes from ours. "What's wrong with Ketchum's Drugs?" I asked.

"I'm having a bit of a feud with Nathan," she said. Nathan Ketchum spent most of his time picking fights with folks from our town. The subject might change, but Nathan's temperament was always the same.

"What happened?" I asked.

"He hired me to build him a new display case. Nathan asked for maple, I made it out of maple, but when he got the bill, he swore he wanted pine. I had his signature on the work order, but he still argued with me about it, so I loaded it back into my pickup truck and drove it back to my shop."

"What in the world are you going to do with a display case?" I asked her.

Emily laughed. "I'll sell it back to him once he cools off, but in the meantime, I'm avoiding his place."

"What's the sheriff's story?" I asked. I had to wonder what would make our chief law enforcement officer abandon one of our local shopkeepers.

"He was in no mood to answer my question when I asked him the same thing, but I think Nathan Ketchum is planning on running for sheriff next election," Emily said. "I can be there within the hour, if you'd like."

"That would be super."

"Great. I'll see you then. By the way, I never told you how sorry I was about Cora and Midnight."

"I appreciate it," I said. "I'll see you soon."

I was a big fan of Emily's, but her last words stung a little. I knew that by opening the shop, I'd be getting a great many more sentiments from friends of Cora's, but I wasn't looking forward to any of it. I knew everyone meant well, but nothing they could say could ease the pain of my losses. I still had Midnight, at least a shadow of him, but that didn't mitigate all of my anguish.

It was finally time to open Memories and Dreams, and with some trepidation, I approached the front door and unlocked it.

I wasn't sure why I'd been so worried about facing the public.

No one was there.

Was this going to be what it was like now that Cora was gone? The fact that she'd been murdered in the shop might just be enough to keep people away, and without customers, I might as well shut the place down right now. It wouldn't be the worst thing in the world that ever happened, but then again, Cora had entrusted me with carrying on, and I was going to do it if I could.

Chapter 6

Emily came in fifteen minutes later, looked around the empty store, and asked with a smile, "Are you sure you're open, Christy?" She was my age, lean and fit, with her brown hair in a constant ponytail, usually sticking out of the back of a baseball cap. The teams and themes changed with the cap of the day, but her smile rarely did. Her current cap was dark blue and sported gold stitching and lettering celebrating the Blue Ridge Parkway, a driving National Park that was one of my favorite places. The narrow ribbon of road ran through some of the prettiest countryside anywhere in the world, and I loved driving on it in just about any season of the year.

"I am, at least in theory. I like your hat."

She nodded. "Thanks. I picked it up last week. Now, let's see about that door." As she started toward the back with her toolbox in one hand, she asked, "Are you sure you can spare the time to show me the problem?"

"I'll manage somehow," I answered with the hint of a grin.

As we got to the door to the storeroom, I reached out and steadied some boxes that always seemed to want to fall over every time I walked through the door. "Want me to help you move some of those so they don't fall and kill somebody?" Emily asked.

"No, I'll take care of it later. Thanks, anyway."

"Just let me know," Emily said, and then she studied the broken back door, carefully removing the plywood the sheriff's deputies had installed temporarily. "I can fix this," she said after a moment's thought.

"There's no doubt in my mind about it," I replied. "I'm not sure what kind of budget I'm working with right now, but I'll find a way to pay you."

"There's no hurry," she said, forgetting for the moment

about the billing and focusing instead on the best way to patch the door. "If we have to, we can work something out in trade, if you're willing."

I looked around the shop. "What on earth do we have that might be of interest to you?" I asked.

"You'd be surprised," was all that she'd say. "I need to take a few measurements and then head back to my shop. You're not going anywhere anytime soon, are you?"

"You don't have to worry about me. I'll be right here," I said.

"Good. I'll see you soon."

Emily ducked out the back and I relocked the door as best I could. I doubted that it would keep an earnest field mouse out, but I didn't believe that whoever had broken in would try to come back during regular business hours. Just in case, though, I promised myself to keep my eyes open for something, anything, that didn't feel right.

An older man I'd seen in the shop a few times before came in through the front door and looked around. I was bent over near the register rearranging a display of costume jewelry and out of sight. "Welcome back," I said.

He looked confused as he glanced around the open space. "Hello? Where are you? I can't see you."

"That's because I was hiding," I said with a slight smile.

He looked surprised by my answer. "Really? Why on earth would you want to do that? Where's the proprietor of this establishment?"

"You're looking at her," I said. It was evident that this man hadn't had a sense of whimsy for years.

"No, I'm talking about the older woman who helped me the last time I was here. It was just last week. Surely you haven't been in charge all that long."

"I'm afraid that Cora is no longer running Memories and Dreams. Was there something that I could help you with?"

"I can't imagine why she would be dismissed. She was a perfectly lovely woman, and she was extremely helpful every time I came in."

This wasn't going to be easy, but I couldn't tap-dance around the issue much longer. "I'm sorry to tell you this, but I'm afraid that she passed away suddenly last week," I said simply.

That took him aback. "I'm so sorry. It must have been sudden. I wasn't even aware of the fact that she was ill."

"She wasn't," I said. "Someone broke into the shop and killed her. They killed my cat, too." I could have been a little more delicate about it, but I'd already tried that route.

"I beg your forgiveness," he said, clearly upset by the news. "This must be a trying time for you."

I never should have been so blunt with him. What had I been thinking? "I'm the one who should be apologizing. To be honest with you, I'm still coming to grips with it myself. It was tragic, but we all have to move on sometime, don't we? Now, was there something in particular that I could help you with?"

"She showed me an array of handcrafted wooden boxes the last time I was here, and I had trouble making up my mind which one I wanted, but I've decided now, and I've come back for it."

We had an assortment of boxes, wooden and otherwise, and since Cora had been killed, only one was missing now, and it was in my jacket pocket. Hopefully, that wouldn't be the one that had caught his eye. "They're in the case over there, if you'll just follow me," I said.

I approached the case and opened it with the special key that fit the cylindrical lock. "Which one would you like to see?"

He leaned over the case, his finger poised to point, when he frowned slightly. "It's not there."

"Could you tell me a little about what it looked like?" I asked, knowing too well which box he was about to describe to me.

Of course, he described my box to a T.

"Sorry, but it's no longer for sale," I said.

"But how can that be? It was priced too high for the common collector, and Cora assured me that in all likelihood, it would be here when I returned."

"I'm sure she was sincere, but you never know, do you? We have some other choices that are quite lovely."

The man frowned. "But I wanted that one in particular. This might be unusual, but could you tell me who might have purchased it? I'd be willing to pay them more than they gave your former employer for it."

"Sorry, but our records are confidential," I said, which in part was true. I knew full well where that box was, but no amount of money would pry it out of my hands after Midnight had directed me to choose it.

"That's unfortunate," he said as he pulled a slim wallet out of his coat pocket. Removing a business card, he slid it across the counter to me as he said, "If the new owner returns, please have them get in touch with me. I'd be willing to make it worth their while."

I dutifully took the card, and then I glanced at the name embossed on it. "Professor Jenkins, may I ask you why you didn't buy it before, if you're willing to pay more than it's worth now?"

"I had to get approval from my wife," he said sheepishly. "She indulges me in my habit of collecting Americana, and that box was a perfect example of primitive artistry."

So, perhaps Midnight had better taste than I did, but I had a hunch that my ghost cat hadn't been interested in that box for any reason other than the messages I'd found there.

"I just had another thought," he said. "If you would be so kind as to get in touch with the buyer and make my proposal for me, I would be most generous in my thanks. We could call it a brokerage fee, or whatever you'd like, and it would be in cash. I simply must have that box, no matter what it costs."

"I'm not sure that I can help you, but I'll do my best," I said.

The professor nodded, and then he left the shop. How

odd. I started to wonder if perhaps I'd been too rash turning him away. After all, once I got the two messages from it, or specifically, one message and one poem, what was the box worth to me? But how could I be certain that I'd found all of the significance that Midnight had seen in it? No, it was better to pass up a big sale than to lose something that meant so much to my ghost cat that it had caused him to come back from wherever cats went once they were gone.

All in all, it was an odd exchange, but then again, working at Memories and Dreams, more of our interactions with customers were more unusual than most other secondhand stores likely ever encountered.

It was nice to see a friendly face the next time someone walked through my door. "Hey, Trudy. How are you?"

"If I were any happier, they'd be tempted to arrest me," the librarian said with a broad smile, and then checked it down immediately. "I apologize, Christy. I shouldn't have said that. I'm sorry for your loss."

"Please, don't apologize for being yourself. It's nice to see someone who isn't tiptoeing around me as though I might shatter at the wrong word." Trudy Jefferson was our town's librarian, number one researcher, and a collector of scarves of all types and kinds. "We just got the coolest scarf in last week," I said. "I put it aside for you so you could have the first look at it."

"That's wonderful," she said as I brought it out from under the counter and handed it over. It was piece of material so fine and delicate that it hardly had any weight in my hand. The colors were translucent and undulating, and it looked as though it would be something that my friend would covet if she saw someone wearing it on the street. Trudy studied it carefully, clearly liking what she saw, and then she draped it over her head and stroked it lightly.

"It's absolutely exquisite," she said. "How much are you asking for it?"

"Just this once, I'll let it go for what we paid for it, since you're such a good customer," I said.

"Nonsense. I'll pay full retail, and be happy for the opportunity to do it."

I smiled at her response, and then I quoted her the price Cora and I had agreed on when it had come in. I would miss that back and forth that my boss and I had when we priced items. I'd been wildly random when Cora had first started training me, but lately our prices matched within pennies, something that I took a great deal of pride in.

"It's worth every cent," she said as she paid me.

"Would you like a bag for it?" I asked as I handed her change to her.

"I believe I'll wear it out of the shop," she said. "How does it look?"

"Smashing," I said with a smile. Trudy was one of the reasons I'd grown to love working at Memories and Dreams, and she'd chosen the perfect time to come in today. I'd needed her smile desperately to remind me why I was doing this.

"I got your panel," Emily said as she came back into the shop a little later. "It will fit like a glove. I promise you."

"Excellent," I said.

Emily frowned for a moment as she looked around. "This still won't take the place of a security system; you know that, don't you?"

"I can't afford much more than the panel replacement," I said. "Cora always talked about getting an alarm for the shop, but she never managed to get far enough ahead."

"They are more reasonable than you might think," Emily said. She studied the door in back, as well as the windows up front and that door. "I can rig something up using items available off the shelf. It won't be too bad."

"Hang on," I said, suddenly unwilling to let the place go unguarded any longer than I had to. "Let me call my financial advisor and see what kind of spending limit I have."

"Sure thing," Emily said, clearly amused by the prospect

of me having someone advising me. "Just let me know. Things are slow right now, so I can jump right on it after I fix the door, if you'd like."

I called Lincoln's office, and to my delight, he took my call straightaway. "I thought you'd be harder to get in touch with than that," I said.

"Usually I would be, but the judge got sick at the last minute, and everything got postponed. How are things going at the store?"

"I'm managing," I said.

"That's wonderful news," he replied.

"Listen, the reason I'm calling is that I was wondering if I had a budget."

"Do you mean money for your own personal use?" he asked. Was that a hint of disappointment in his voice? Somehow, that thought bothered me.

"It's for the shop, actually. My handywoman is here, and she says that she can rig up an alarm that won't cost too much. I feel kind of naked without something here protecting the place, to be honest with you."

"If she can keep it under three hundred dollars, I can approve it," Lincoln said.

"It's really going to be that easy?" I asked, a little surprised by how simply the request had been fulfilled.

"Just don't get carried away," Lincoln said. "You have a little room, but the less ammo we give the cousins for any potential court fight, the better off we'll be."

"How can they complain if I'm just trying to protect their assets?" I asked.

"The assets under your control aren't theirs yet," Lincoln reminded me. "You're in the driver's seat right now." I couldn't even let myself entertain that thought. As a matter of fact, it helped thinking that I was just there to run the place temporarily, not working to earn the lion's share of it. In my mind, it was as though Cora had stepped out for a long lunch, and she'd be back anytime. I knew deep down that this wasn't going to happen, but that didn't keep me from lying to myself that it was a possibility.

"Thanks," I said, and then I hung up. Emily was putting the finishing touches on the new door panel, and if I hadn't known that she'd just replaced the kicked-in panel, I never would have been able to spot it. "That looks great," I said.

She wiped a spot of glue off the panel with a wet rag, and then she examined the patch. "It'll do, if I do say so myself. I'm just about finished here. Have you had a chance to think about an alarm system?"

"How much money are we talking here?" I asked, not willing to share my budget restrictions with her if I didn't have to.

"I can do a nice little system for five hundred bucks," she said.

My face fell. "I'm sorry. That's way over my head. It'll just have to wait for better days. Thanks for offering, though."

"Hang on. We're just getting started with the negotiation," Emily said with a grin. "I quoted you the price for a system with cameras at the front and the back, along with remote controls so you could turn everything on and off on the Internet without ever leaving the house."

"How about the stripped down version?" I asked.

"Well, for a hundred and a half, I can wire the doors and windows with a siren that will wake the dead. No cameras, though."

"How about splitting the difference? What will three hundred buy me?"

She thought about it, jotted some numbers down in the same notebook where she'd recorded the dimensions to my door patch, and then said, "I can wire the doors and windows and give you one camera. It won't cover the entire place, but it will be loads better than not having anything at all. That price includes a digital recorder, too, something we can hide out of sight in case a burglar discovers the camera and tries to remove the evidence. That money will also get you enough signage around the shop that you'll most likely scare off any but the hardiest thief."

I thought about it for two seconds, but there really wasn't that much to weigh in making the decision. Lincoln had given me the go ahead, and by golly, I was going to go ahead. "How soon can you get started?"

Emily smiled broadly when she heard the news. "Good for you. I can get started this evening after you close for the day, and I'll have you operational by midnight."

I must have flinched at my cat's name. Emily frowned, clearly misunderstanding my disapproval. "Would eleven be better? What time do you close, anyway?"

"Cora kept us open until six, and to be honest with you, I don't see any reason to change our hours, at least not just yet."

"Perfect. I'll pick up everything I need, grab a quick bite, and then be back here by six p.m. sharp."

"Thanks, Emily. I really appreciate your help."

"I'm happy to do it," she said as she gathered her tools and left. She was, as my late father used to say, good people, and I felt deep in my heart that I could trust her. My instincts were rarely wrong when it came to people, and the few times that I'd been disappointed, I hadn't let it get me down for too long. I was trusting Emily not just to set up an alarm system for me at a fair price, but I was also going to leave her alone in the shop without me. I couldn't imagine her stealing from me, or from Cora's estate. But if she did, it would be on her conscience, not mine.

That was fine, as far as it went, but was it right that I was about to trust her with things that weren't mine, at least completely? I decided to call Lincoln back to get his approval. I was finding that working in a store and running it were two entirely different things, and I wasn't all that certain that I was ready, or even interested, in the added responsibilities.

"Two calls, back to back. I'm honored," Lincoln said when he picked up.

"Do you know Emily Nance very well?" I asked him.

"We went to high school together," Lincoln admitted. "Why?"

"She's going to install my burglar alarm system tonight after hours," I explained. "Is it okay to trust her here alone in the shop?"

"I'd trust the woman with my life. Why, did you get a different read on her?"

"No, I trusted her from the moment we met. I just realized that maybe my opinion wasn't enough anymore."

Lincoln laughed a little, so I asked, "What's so funny?"

"Nothing. It's really true that heavy is the head that wears the crown."

"Don't go quoting Shakespeare to me, Counselor, but if you do, the least you could do is to get it right," I said with a slight smile. "The quote is, 'Uneasy lies the head that wears a crown.'"

"Are you certain about that?"

"Check me if you'd like. It's from Henry the Fourth, Part 2."

"No, I believe you. You never cease to amaze me, Christy."

I had to laugh at that. "I don't see how. Look at how far I've fallen, from dedicated scholar all the way down to common clerk."

"You're much more than that, and there's nothing about you that's common," he said. "But to answer your question, yes, I trust Emily Nance."

"That's good enough for me, then. Thanks, Lincoln."

The attorney hesitated, and then he asked timidly, "Do you have any interest in going out to dinner with me tonight? You've had a particularly difficult day, and you should celebrate."

"It's sweet of you to offer, but honestly, I just want to go home after I turn the key over to Emily and sleep until it's time to get up tomorrow."

"I understand completely," he said, though it was pretty clear that I'd hurt his feelings.

"I'll take a rain check, though, if you're offering one. Any other time, dinner out sounds great."

"You've got it," he said, noticeably perking up. "Just name the time and the place, and I'll be there."

"Will do," I said. After we hung up, it suddenly occurred to me that I'd just made a date with Marybeth's former flame. What had I been thinking? I considered calling him back and canceling, but honestly, we'd left it wide open, and nothing said that I had to cash the rain check that he'd given me. I had too much on my mind at the moment, and too much sadness in my heart, to start dating, so for now, I'd just leave things as they stood.

Though I had a few other shoppers come into Memories and Dreams in the course of the rest of the day, I didn't make any major sales, or purchases, either. We bought things from folks who walked in off the street, but most of our items were bought on one of Cora's buying trips, something she called scavenger hunts. Twice a year, armed with a healthy budget and a panel van, Cora took two weeks off looking for unique items to stock the store. She'd taken me along when I'd first gone to work with her, and the trip had cemented our friendship, even though I'd desperately missed my cats. Sharing a room wherever we stopped, Cora had been so different from her daily work persona—looser, friendlier, and much funnier. Another trip was scheduled for next month, but I wasn't sure I could do it by myself. It wouldn't be the same without her, and I wasn't about to leave Shadow behind, or Midnight either, for that matter. We'd just have to see. I kept hoping to get a glimpse of Midnight as I walked through the store, but he didn't make another appearance. I wasn't sure what his manifestations were costing him in energy or whatever ran his existence now, but it couldn't have been that easy for him.

I was ten minutes from closing, and there was still no sign of Emily. Had she gotten held up on another job? No, a minute later, she showed up, along with a mass of boxes and tools loaded on a cart that she pushed ahead of her.

"Admit it. You didn't think I was coming, did you?" she asked with a grin.

"That's a lot of stuff," I said as I surveyed her load.

"We got lucky. I found some of the hardware I needed on sale, so this is going to cost you sixty dollars less than I quoted you."

"Hey, I'll take anything I can get," I said. "Thanks for passing the savings along to me."

Emily smiled. "We're both going to come out ahead on this deal now. I love sharing my good fortune. How was your afternoon?"

"It was slow," I said. "But that's about what I expected. I'm not sure how many of our old customers are going to come back after what happened here."

"Give them a little time, Christy. They won't desert you."

"I hope you're right," I said. "Are you going to install all of that by yourself? Is there anybody you can call for help?"

"Honestly, I'd rather work alone. No one else seems to be able to meet my standards. Are you okay with leaving me here all by myself? I know that you don't really know me all that well, so if you're nervous about leaving me here unsupervised, I totally get it."

"Don't worry. You had some good references. I trust you."

She looked at me curiously. "Do you mind if I ask who exactly it was who vouched for me?"

I couldn't imagine Lincoln having a problem with me disclosing his identity. "I called Lincoln Hayes."

Emily's grin broadened. "He's a good guy, isn't he?"

"That's what I keep hearing," I said. "Marybeth vouched for him, and now he's vouching for you."

"You must really trust Marybeth," she said.

"With my life, and with my cat," I said, nearly failing to make it singular instead of plural. That got me thinking about Midnight again, and I wondered briefly if I should warn Emily that Midnight might show up while she was working. No, it would serve only to make me look as though I'd lost my mind. If she saw my ghost cat, I hoped that she'd tell me about it. Maybe I'd even ask her in a roundabout way if he made an appearance while she was working. I had a sudden thought. Emily was putting in a surveillance camera. Would his ghostly image show up on tape? Having proof that he was actually there, and not some figment of my imagination, would be vastly reassuring, but then again, I didn't expect it to capture his essence. Midnight had been rather hard to photograph while he'd been alive, and I suspected that his ghost wouldn't be any more cooperative than he'd been in real life.

I handed Emily a piece of paper that I'd prepared for her. "Here's my cell number, and Marybeth's home number. If you need anything, don't hesitate to call either number."

"What should I do when I'm finished?" she asked. "Do you want me to drop your key off at the house, or should I meet you here tomorrow morning when you're ready to open?"

"I have another key at home. Just lock up when you're finished, and I'll get it back from you later. How's that sound?"

"Like you really do trust me," she said. "Don't worry. I won't let you down."

"I believe you," I said, and then I left her there, already buried in packaging, hardware, and a layout she'd sketched on the back of a fast food bag. There was something about the young woman that exuded competence.

Without a single glance back, I walked out the door and headed home.

Chapter 7

"When are you coming home?" Marybeth asked me after I answered her call on the way home.

"I'm on my way right now. Why, what's up?"

"Would you mind swinging by the pizza place and picking up the order I just placed? Don't worry, it's not another pizza. I ordered us some mozzarella and cinnamon sticks this time."

"Mozzarella and cinnamon together? That doesn't sound like a very good combination to me."

"They are separate and you know it, you ninny," she said with a laugh. "I'm going to change out of this suit while you're running our errands and get myself into something a lot grubbier."

"Happy to do it," I said.

"Does that mean that you've finally got your appetite back?" Marybeth asked. "How was your French toast this morning?"

I decided not to tell her yet about Jim Hicks and his desire to take my shop over. "It was delicious, and yes, I seem to be eating again. Why don't you pick out a sappy romantic movie we can watch tonight? It will be like college all over again."

"Great minds think alike. I've got one queued up right now, along with half a gallon of mint chocolate chip ice cream for dessert. We are getting into a time machine tonight of food, fun, and no boys allowed."

I thought about telling her about my tentative date with her ex-boyfriend, but that was something else that could wait, since Lincoln and I hadn't set anything in stone. "I'm on board. See you soon."

I walked in the door ten minutes later, balancing the food in one arm as I got out my keys and opened the door.

"Food's here," I yelled as I walked in.

Shadow must have thought that I was talking to him. He came down the hallway, and to my surprise, he leapt into my arms, nearly knocking the box out of my hands. "Hey, what's going on, big guy?" I asked as I set the box down and gave him my undivided attention. It was rare that he showed such overt enthusiasm for my appearance, and I had to wonder if he was still a little more rattled by Midnight's sudden reappearance than he'd let on. Shadow allowed himself to be held, and then drove his head gently into my neck as I rubbed his. After a minute of reassurance, he shook his head, sneezed once, and then he leapt back down to the floor. The fluidity of my cats had always impressed me, and I wished that I was one tenth as limber as they were.

"Did I hear someone promise me food?" Marybeth asked as she came downstairs. Gone was her suit, replaced by a faded pair of sweatpants with UNC-A running down one leg, and a sweatshirt that had belonged to one of her college boyfriends. He'd wanted it back when they'd broken up, but Marybeth had claimed it as a spoil of war since he'd cheated on her, and even worse, she'd caught him red-handed.

"How can you wear that after what Lee did you?"

"Hey, it's the most comfortable thing I've ever owned. Besides, I smile whenever I put it on. He offered me a hundred bucks to get it back after we broke up. That makes it the most valuable sweatshirt I've ever owned."

"Your logic is seriously flawed, you know that, don't you?" I asked her with a grin.

"Hey, it makes sense in my world. What else matters? Now, are we going to eat and lose ourselves in a sappy movie, or what? I've already opened the wine, and the movie's ready to play."

"Let's do it," I said. A girl's night was exactly what I needed to take my mind off things. It was one more reason Marybeth was so important in my life. She'd seen the need for an escape in me, and then she'd taken steps to make it happen.

As we ate, Shadow came in, sniffed at my pizza stick, and then settled down in my lap. I stroked him as I watched, and when I looked up, Marybeth was staring at me. "What? Do I have pizza sauce on my chin or something?"

"You really miss Midnight, don't you?"

"We both do," I said as I stroked Shadow again. "Don't you?"

"Of course I do. The rascal had a larger than life presence, you know? I half expect him to show up again at the oddest times."

I nearly asked her, "You haven't seen him since he died, have you?" but I kept it to myself. This evening was going too well to mess it up by making Marybeth think that I was crazy. "Me, too," was all that I said.

Shadow had clearly had enough of being fussed over. He stood, stretched as only a cat could, and then went off in search of something more exciting. Was Midnight waiting for him somewhere else in the house? The thought made me want to get up and look for him myself, but I couldn't figure out a way to do it without making Marybeth suspicious. Besides, I was beginning to think that he wouldn't show up unless I was alone, even if no one else *could* see him. At least that had been my experience so far. Then again, he hadn't been around all that often, so I wasn't exactly sure what rules governed him at the moment.

Later that night as I settled into sleep, I heard a gentle purring beside me, and extending my hand without another thought, I started stroking the cat nearby.

The only problem was that my hand went right through him. Midnight was back, and he seemed to take some comfort from my presence. That was only fair, since I was taking a great deal from his.

"I miss you," I whispered softly to him.

In response, he tried his best to rub his head against me, but it was to no avail.

"Merwr," he said in that wistful way of his when he

realized that he was going to have to be content with the status quo.

"At least you're here," I said, and with the last word I spoke, he disappeared again. It tore me up losing him, but in some ways, his partial presence was even harder on me. I wanted to be able to stroke his neck, tickle his chin, and bump heads with him, but the most he could muster was an ethereal presence in my life. Was it better than nothing? In many ways, yes, but in some, it only served to remind me just what I'd lost. Shadow jumped up on the bed and did his best to greet me in his most open fashion, and it helped a lot.

"Mwrerewr," he said.

"I know. It's hard, isn't it?" I asked.

"Mwer," he replied. Midnight had been a no-nonsense kind of cat, while Shadow had always been the sentimental one of the pair. I rubbed his head once, and then I tried to go to sleep. I was resolved now, more than ever, to find Midnight's killer, and Cora's too, of course.

It was the least I could do for my two lost friends.

At least I didn't get any telephone calls in the middle of the night, whether it was due to Emily's excellent work, or the fact that the killer might have already got what they'd been after. I doubted it was the latter, though. The shop had looked like I'd interrupted someone before they found what they'd been looking for. At least I hoped that was the case.

There was a note downstairs from Marybeth when I walked into the kitchen. "Gone to Charlotte. Back tonight. Japanese tonight?"

I took a quick shower, got dressed, and then headed over to Memories and Dreams. I had over an hour to check over the stock for something valuable that Cora and I might have missed. Why else would the killer have returned to the scene of the crime?

If there was something of great intrinsic value there, I couldn't find it. Our things were mostly nice, sometimes quirky, and often unique, but if there was a hidden gem among the rest of our inventory, I didn't have an eye educated enough to spot it. It was time to give up the search, at least for now. And where was Cora's notebook? It had contained some pretty explosive claims about several people I knew, and I didn't want it falling into the wrong hands. What had Cora been thinking, speculating about so much, and then writing her wild guesses down on paper? It had been a dangerous hobby, especially if the book found itself in the wrong hands. A sudden thought occurred to me. Could *that* have been the reason for the break-in, and *not* a robbery, as everyone suspected? I decided to make a serious attempt to find that notebook, but for now, I had more pressing work on my mind.

Exactly at ten o'clock, I opened the shop to find an older man wearing a threadbare suit and battered wingtips that hadn't seen a buffing cloth in years. He clutched a worn old leather briefcase as though it were a life preserver.

"May I help you?" I asked. "Is there something in particular that you're looking for?"

"Are you Christine Blake?" he asked.

"I go by Christy, but yes, that's my legal name," I said. "Why do you ask?"

"I am Caleb Wright. I represent Sandy and Mandy Anthony," he said.

I couldn't help the frown that suddenly appeared on my face. "I can't imagine what you'd want to discuss with me."

"I am here to inform you that my clients are contesting the alleged last will and testament of their cousin, Cora Anthony."

"On what grounds?" I asked, disappointed, though not surprised, by their move.

"Forgive me," he said as his hands shook a little, "but they are challenging the provisions of Ms. Anthony's will that leave the lion's share of the business to you."

"I had no idea they were all that interested in the place," I said. "With all due respect, I've been working here for quite a long time, and they've never come by the shop, not even once."

"Whatever the case might be, they are quite eager to visit now," he said.

"According the will, though, that's not an option, is it?"

"We feel that you may have exerted undue influence over Ms. Anthony," he said as though he were scolding me like a small and unruly child.

I'd had just about enough of that. "I believe you should discuss this further with my attorney."

"I'd be delighted. Who might that be?" he asked.

"Surely the sisters must have told you. It's Lincoln Hayes," I said. Mr. Wright seemed to recoil at my attorney's name. "Do you know him?" I asked.

"No, but I certainly know of him," Mr. Wright said. "I do hope he won't be too difficult in this matter."

"I don't know any other way to say this without sounding disrespectful, but I hope he *will* be, with all my heart."

The aging attorney looked startled by my admission. "If you're going to take that tone, I believe this interview is over."

"I believe that it is," I said. "I'd wish you a nice day, but I hate to say things that I don't mean."

After he was gone, I picked up the telephone and called Lincoln. His secretary put me straight through, and when he answered, I said, "I just had a visit from an attorney named Caleb Wright. Do you know him?"

"I've seen him around the courthouse. What did he want with you?"

"He informed me that Cora's cousins weren't all that happy with her will. They are planning to contest it. They're going to claim that I exerted undue influence over Cora."

"Why am I not surprised that they'd feel that way?" Lincoln asked a little sadly.

"Should I be worried?" I asked. I still wasn't one hundred percent certain that I wanted Dreams and Memories, but that didn't mean that I was willing to stand by while someone else stole it out from under me.

"There's absolutely no justification for their position," he said.

"You didn't answer my question."

"Christy, judges have minds of their own, so I can't say with complete certainty that this is going to just go away, but I'm as sure as I can be that we'll beat them. We just have to stand firm and respect Cora's wishes. If they see that we aren't going to fold under their threats, I'm fairly certain they will just give up."

"I hope you are right. No matter what happens with this trial run, *I* want to be the one who makes the decision whether I move on or not, do you know what I mean?"

"I do, and I applaud your spirit. I'd be delighted to give Mr. Wright a call for you, if you'd like."

"Thank you, but no. Let's leave things in their court for now, shall we?"

"I think that's an excellent idea. Now, if there's nothing else that's pressing, I need to be in court in ten minutes."

"Sorry for the interruption," I said.

"Feel free to call me anytime," he said, and then Lincoln hung up.

"Can I help you with anything in particular?" I asked a nicely dressed man somewhere in his fifties a little later that day. He'd come into the shop and had headed straight to our jewelry counter. He was still leaning over and peering inside when I approached him. We kept lots of old pieces on display there: rings, necklaces, brooches, cameos, and more. Most of the items were vintage, but a few were newer, cast-offs that the original owner had lost interest in. We weren't a pawn shop, and no one turned to us for brief loans, but we did buy things we thought we could resell, and that included a rather nice collection of gold and silver jewelry.

He looked startled as I spoke, so I said, "Sorry to sneak up on you like that. What exactly were you looking for?"

"Cora's got something of mine, and I want it back," he

said loudly. If anyone else had been in the shop, it would have clearly captured their attention, but for once, having an empty store was a good thing.

I took a deep breath, and then I asked, "Would you mind being a little more specific? What exactly are we talking about here?"

"It's a necklace about this big," he said as he showed me his index finger and thumb spaced about three inches apart. "It had a large 'C' engraved on it, and you wouldn't be likely to mistake it for anything else. I don't see it in the case, though."

I had to fight the temptation to be sure that my necklace was safely tucked inside my blouse. I had no idea what this man was talking about, and it was going to take more than a wild accusation for him to get his hands on my prize. "As you can see, it's no longer here," I said.

"Of course I can see that," he said, and though he didn't call me an idiot outright, it was pretty clearly implied in the emphatic way he'd spoken. "What I want to know is where it is now."

I held up one finger. "Let me consult our records." He may have been under the impression that I was looking up the new owner's contact information, but I didn't really have to do that. What I wanted to check on was how the necklace had come into the shop in the first place. I opened our ledger of purchases, checked the jewelry section, and soon had the original owner's vital information at my fingertips. Our filing system wasn't computerized, cross-referenced, or searchable by tapping a few keys, but I'd found it fast enough under Cora's system, not that a stranger would have been able to do it. Cora's system was unique, and virtually undecipherable by the common layman, but I'd had the advantage of working at the shop for quite some time under her tutelage.

I turned the book around and emphasized the entry I'd just found with my finger. "It says here that the necklace in question was purchased for one hundred dollars cash from

Eleanor Whitman on September nineteenth of this year."

"I know who sold it," he said angrily. "I'm her son, David. My mother had no right to sell it, and Cora Anthony had even less right to purchase it."

"Are you claiming that the necklace was stolen?" I asked earnestly. Buying stolen goods was a huge no-no in our business, and if we'd purchased something that hadn't belonged to the seller, the police would confiscate the item without recompense to us. That meant that we not only lost the value of the necklace and the opportunity to resell it, but it also meant that we were out our initial payment. It was something that Cora had taken very seriously, as did I.

"No, of course not. It was a present from my father to my mother. She owned it outright."

"Then she had every right to sell it," I said.

"For a hundred measly dollars? Believe me, it was worth substantially more than that amount."

I turned the book back around and studied the entry again. There was a wavy symbol beside the dollar amount, another part of Cora's bookkeeping code. "It says here that was all your mother asked for when she came in, and Cora paid her the full amount. I don't see that you have a right to it now, based on what you just told me. Our policy is, and always has been, no refunds or exchanges. All sales and purchases are final." I pointed to the sign posted just below the register, and I was glad that Cora had insisted that it always be displayed prominently.

"Yeah, well, your boss took advantage of her," he said, this time with more vehemence.

"I'm sorry that you're unhappy with the transaction. If your mother would like to come in and lodge a protest of her own, I'd be happy to explain our policies to her as well."

"She doesn't even realize that she was cheated," he said angrily.

"Then I'm afraid that I can't help you," I explained.

He looked around wildly, and then back at me. "This isn't the end of this."

I decided to keep my mouth shut as he stormed out of the shop. It was one of the downsides of owning a small business, dealing with customers who were unhappy with their earlier decisions. Cora had told me that she'd adopted the No Refunds, No Returns policy for sales and purchases early on after first opening the shop. It made things that could have been complicated much simpler. The meaning of the sign was clear. Make up your mind before you buy or sell, because there's no going back. It was a policy I heartily approved of, and I had no plan to ever change.

I was still wondering if he was going to come back and take another run at me when someone else walked in instead.

This day was getting more complicated by the minute, and I was beginning to regret unlocking the doors in the first place when Jim Hicks, the real estate agent who wanted to buy Memories and Dreams, walked into my shop.

Chapter 8

"I hope you didn't come by to chat about your offer," I said before the agent could say a single word. "I've just gone round and round with a belligerent customer, so I'm not feeling particularly hospitable at the moment, particularly if you're here to ask me to sell the place."

Hicks pursed his lips, blew out a little air, and then offered me a smile, which was quite startling. "I understand completely. We all have days like that. I'll see you tomorrow," he said as he turned on his heels and left.

His reaction surprised me so much that I burst out laughing as soon as he was gone, and I was still chuckling a little when Celeste from next door walked in.

"Did I just see Jim Hicks heading in here?" she asked, and then she must have noticed that I was laughing. "What's so funny? That man is not known for his humorous nature, if you know what I mean."

"It's too difficult to explain without going into a whole lot of backstory," I said, not wanting to get into any long and drawn out conversations about my day. "What can I do for you, Celeste?"

"I was just checking up on you," she asked as she looked around the shop. "How has your first full day on your own been so far?"

"It was about what I expected," I said, though that was far from the truth. "Thanks for asking, though."

"You know, if running this shop gets to be too overwhelming, there *are* other alternatives," she said.

"Well, I can't afford to hire anyone else at the moment on my limited budget," I said. "Frankly, I'm not sure how Cora could ever afford my paycheck, as lean as it was."

"I wasn't volunteering for a job," she said. "What I'm saying is that I might be able to take this place off your hands, if it would help you out. I've been thinking about expanding the café, but with the bank being directly on the other side of me, this is the only way I can increase my square footage. I'm already blocked in by the streets in front and in back."

"I had no idea you needed more space," I said.

"I keep thinking that I'm missing an opportunity here," she said. "Cora and I even discussed it a time or two. As a matter of fact, I was caught off guard when I found out that she ended up leaving this place to you. I thought we had an agreement, at least in principal, that when she left the shop, I'd have first rights to buy the space."

That was interesting, since Cora had never breathed one word about it to me. "Trust me. Her arrangements caught me by surprise as well," I said.

"Still, it's a lot to ask of you to keep the place running on your own," Celeste said.

"Oh, I'm not alone."

"Really?" Celeste asked as she looked around. "I had no idea that anyone else was here."

"I'm not talking about employees," I said. "I mean my friends."

Celeste nodded, and then she added a smile. "Friends can be the greatest assets we have. Well, it sounds as though you're doing just fine on your own, so I won't bother you about it anymore." Celeste looked around the shop, and then she asked me, "Have you been able to track down Cora's notebook yet?"

"You know about that, do you?" I asked.

Celeste waved a hand in the air. "Most folks in town knew about her journal. Cora had some pretty wild ideas about some of the folks around here, but I always figured that it was mostly just idle speculation."

"I haven't seen it since I took over," I said honestly, though it was true that I'd been searching for it. Was it possible that Celeste was asking because her name might have been in it?

"It doesn't matter," she said as she waved a hand in the

air. "I'd just hate to see it fall into the wrong hands. Now remember, if you need anything, I'm right next door. I'll be disappointed if I discover that you were in need of assistance and didn't call on me."

"Thanks. I'll keep that in mind," I said.

Celeste nodded. "Excellent. Now, if you'll excuse me, I'd better get back to work before Hester burns the place down. We can't have that, now can we? That would make us both homeless. Will I see you at breakfast tomorrow morning?"

"I haven't decided yet," I answered honestly.

"Well, you always know where to find me," she said, and with that, she was gone. Celeste's offer to buy me out had been odd, but what had really struck me was the way she'd hinted around about Cora's journal. It just doubled my desire to read the thing carefully and see who exactly was mentioned in it, and what they had been up to that merited their entry.

All in all, though, I'd had just about all of the questions I could take for the day, no matter how good the intentions were of the folks who'd been grilling me. I made an executive decision, flipped over the OPEN sign to CLOSED, and started getting ready to go home. The first thing I did to signify that we were closed for business was to pull the blinds, shutting off most of the outside light that had been coming through the large windows up front.

As I was running the report on the register, I walked through the shop, turning off most of the lights as I went. I was in the back triple-checking the repaired door when Midnight suddenly appeared out of nowhere. "Hello, old friend," I said. I doubted that I'd ever get used to his new status, but I hoped that over time I had the opportunity. Of course, I would have much rather had him with me in whole, but at this point, I would take what I could get.

"Mewr," he said as he looked at me rather impatiently.

"No, I haven't had any luck yet with the clues you pointed out to me. It's not that easy, you know."

He shook his head, and then turned swiftly to show me his tail, a sure sign of his disapproval.

"Excuse me, but I've been kind of busy running the place," I said.

"Mewerwr," he replied as he turned back around and stared at me. Boy, had I ever seen that expression before.

"Okay, there's no need to scold me. I'm doing my best."

As he vanished, I found myself staring at where he'd just been. Midnight had never been the most patient of cats, a species not usually known for their forbearance. He was right, though. I'd spent so much time and energy making sure that the shop was up and running that I hadn't spent much time trying to uncover the identity of the killer. Reaching into my pocket, I again pulled out the poem that Cora had left behind. As I reread the words, I had to wonder just when she'd written them. Did the poem have something to do with the killings? Had Midnight pointed the box out to me to get me to see the threat someone had made against Cora, or to solve the puzzle?

The riches of the world are hidden away,
Masked in the Devil's Light.
A chest of fire burns deep within,
Hiding the heart of Midnight.

I flipped the paper over, and as I held it up to the light to study it closer, I realized that instead of being completely blank, there was a faint imprint hidden there. Something had been written on the sheet before it, and Cora had pressed down hard enough to make an impression. After grabbing a nearby pencil, I turned it on its side and rubbed the lead carefully over the paper. I'd had fun with my friends in grade school passing notes that way, and we'd laughed about our secret code that no one else could read. It appeared to be a note of some sort, but the contents of it weren't what struck me immediately. Cora had used the sheet to write a note to the man who was supposed to fix our furnace, something I still needed to take care of when I got around to it.

What caught my attention was the date on the note. It

matched a date that had been burned into my mind forever, one of major significance to me.

Clearly, Cora had written the poem the day she'd been murdered.

It was indeed a clue to something, but what it might be I didn't know.

I decided to try to break the poem down and see if I could make any sense of it. Maybe if I tried to solve it as though it was just one of my boss's old quizzes, I'd have more luck.

The first line obviously referred to the hidden riches of the world. Did that mean that Cora had hidden something of value that I didn't know about? Or was she talking about something more vague, like friendship? I decided that the *only* way the clues were going to work would be if I made them as literal as I could, so I decided that this was indeed about monetary wealth of some kind. Okay, line two mentioned the devil's light. I looked around the backroom of the shop, wondering what that could mean. Nothing came to mind immediately, so I'd clearly have to give it more thought. The third line mentioned a chest of fire, and I honestly had no idea what that might mean. The fourth line was even more confusing. What had she meant by the heart of Midnight? Had she had a prescient moment about the fate of my cat? None of it made sense, at least not at the moment. As for the stand-alone note I'd found in the box warning Cora that this was her last chance, what could that possibly mean? What exactly was it the last chance for Cora to do?

I was more confused than ever.

In frustration, I called out into the empty room, "I could use a little help here, Midnight. Another clue would be of more use to me than your scolding."

There was no response, or sudden appearance, either.

Why was I not surprised?

As I walked back out front, the lights all dimmed now, I glanced back up at the glowing red exit sign we'd been required to install over the door that led to the storeroom.

That's when I saw it!

How had I missed that before? The 'x' in 'exit' was dark, so the sign read simply 'e it' when examined closely.

Not only could it be the second line's reference to the devil's light, but it also showed up as 'x marks the spot.' Unless I missed my guess, here was my next real clue.

Grabbing a ladder from the back, I set it up and looked behind the sign to see if anything was there. Hopefully there would be a note explaining everything.

I should have been so lucky.

Instead of the hoped-for straightforward clue, all I found was a folded playing card, the Ace of Diamonds to be exact, and a dried up piece of greenery that had faded to brown under the heat from the bulb's light.

What in the world were they supposed to mean?

I examined the dried fern frond first, but I'd never taken any botany classes in college, so if this particular variety had a specific name that might help me solve the puzzle, it was beyond me. I wasn't sure even an expert could help identify it at this point. The fern crumbled at my touch, and there wasn't really enough left for anyone to examine after I'd retrieved it from the exit light. Brushing it off my hands into the trash, I turned to the playing card. There was nothing on the surface of it, written or scratched. After grabbing the magnifying glass Cora kept by the register, I studied both sides of the playing card, but if there was a hidden message there, I couldn't find it.

My former boss had been a little too clever about the last clues she'd ever leave me, and I began to wonder if I'd ever figure out exactly what she'd been trying to tell me.

The register signaled that the report was finished, so I moved the ladder back where it belonged, filled out the deposit slip for the bank, and put the store to bed for the night. Whatever Cora had been trying to tell me, it would have to wait another day. I'd been there all day, and I was ready to get home and get something substantial to eat. My appetite was finally back, and I meant to catch up with the meals that I'd skipped in my grief.

I saw Lincoln's car in the driveway when I got home, and when I walked inside, he was sitting in the living room talking to Marybeth.

"I'm not interrupting anything, am I?" I asked. "If you two want some privacy, I'd be glad to drive around awhile."

Lincoln looked embarrassed by my offer, but the look of distaste on my roommate's face was priceless.

"Ew," she said. "I don't think so."

"Hey, I'm sitting right here," Lincoln said. "You didn't used to find my company so distasteful, or do I need to remind you of our past?"

"Please, that was ancient history. You're solidly in the Friend-Zone now, and I can't imagine you ever escaping."

Lincoln started to get up, but Marybeth put a hand on his arm. "Where do you think you're going?"

"I'm not sure, but it's going to be someplace where pretty girls don't get repulsed by the thought of being out on a date with me," he said.

"Do you honestly think there even *is* such a place?" Marybeth asked him with a laugh. The words would have stung if she hadn't been smiling broadly. It was tough to be mad at her when she grinned, as she full well knew.

"Maybe not," Lincoln said as he settled back down. "To answer your question, Christy, I'm here for you."

"Do you mean you want to have our date *now*?" I asked.

Before he could answer, Marybeth nearly levitated off the couch. "*Excuse* me? When did *this* happen? When did you two decide to finally go out on a date, and why did no one inform me immediately?"

"See. Not every pretty girl finds me repulsive," Lincoln said with a grin of his own.

"Oh hush, you're just fishing for compliments," Marybeth told him. "You know how handsome you are."

"Still, a guy likes to hear it every now and then, just the same," Lincoln said.

"Your vanity will be the death of you yet," Marybeth told

him, and then she turned to look at me. "Now, spill. When did you make a date to go out with my ex-boyfriend?"

"Not so funny now, is it?" Lincoln asked her smugly.

"I'll talk to you in a minute," she said. "Well? I'm listening, Christy."

"It's not what you think," I started to say, and then I saw Lincoln's face fall. "Okay, maybe it is, maybe it isn't, but it's beside the point." I looked into Lincoln's eyes as I said, "We were going to leave it up in the air. That means that I'll let you know when and if I'm ready. I'm not trying to back out of it," I said quickly. "I'm just going to need more time."

He nodded. "I get that completely. I'm not here to pressure you. I ran into Marybeth at the bank, and she suggested that you needed a night out with friends. That's all I'm offering you tonight, unless you want to ramp things up and leave her here."

"I don't. At least not now," I said. Why were my cheeks starting to warm up? Was I actually blushing? Before my roommate could get a wisecrack in, I looked at Marybeth and said slowly and deliberately, "Not One Word. Understood?"

"Understood," she said. "He's right, you know. This is just a proposal that we get you out of the house tonight with some food and maybe even a few laughs. What do you say?"

"As much as I appreciate the thought, I'm beat. I was counting on a long hot bath, a quick bite, and then bed."

Lincoln looked at me and grinned. "Actually, I might be able to help you with at least *some* of that."

Marybeth laughed as she playfully slugged his arm. "Good for you, Tiger. Don't give up that easily. I didn't know you had it in you."

"*I'm* not sure it's all that good," I said.

"Come on, Christy. Grab a shower and change into something nice. This will be good for you," Marybeth said. "And if you don't agree this instant, you know that I'm going to keep hammering away at you until you agree, so you might as well save us both some grief."

I knew firsthand how relentless she could be. "Give me

half an hour," I said.

"You've got twelve minutes," Marybeth said. "Otherwise, this nice young lawyer is going to take me somewhere for dinner that I could never afford on my own."

"I don't know what you're talking about. You make more than I do," Lincoln protested.

"Maybe yes, maybe no, but we both know that you're too much of a Southern gentleman to let me pay."

"Go ahead. Try me," he said with a grin.

"That settles it. Hurry up, Christy. I was just bluffing."

I hurried upstairs and took a quick shower. Maybe they were right. It could be fun going out to eat somewhere where I didn't have to order into a clown's mouth, and it might take my mind off of all that I'd lost all too recently.

Chapter 9

"Wow, are you *sure* you can afford this?" I asked after we were seated in a nice restaurant I'd only heard about from a few of our wealthier customers. It was called Umber, an elegant dining experience that served only the finest food and cocktails.

"Relax and enjoy yourself tonight," Lincoln said. "Don't worry about what anything costs."

"We can split the bill if you'd like," Marybeth said as she touched Lincoln's hand.

"No, that's fine. I just won a big case, so I don't think you'll break me beyond repair. We can call this a celebration, if it will help."

"No offense, but I don't feel like there's all that much for me to be celebrate at the moment," I said.

Lincoln nodded. "I understand completely. How about this? When the wine comes, we toast Midnight's memory. Would that ease your mind?"

"Considerably, but Midnight hated wine."

"Milk, then," Lincoln said.

"He wasn't a fan of that, either. His favorite drink was ginger ale, actually."

"Well, I don't care if it offends his memory, I'm not going to toast him with ginger ale."

"He liked root beer, too," Marybeth added.

"Don't either one of you know that it's bad luck to toast with anything that's not alcoholic?"

"Who came up with that rule?" Marybeth asked.

"Someone who really liked to drink, most likely," Lincoln said.

"Wine would be nice," I said. "I'm sure that Midnight wouldn't mind just this once."

"Then, wine it is," Lincoln said.

As he motioned to a nearby waiter, I spotted someone

across the room. "What is Jim Hicks doing here?" I asked Marybeth.

"I don't know. He really has some kind of nerve, doesn't he?"

"You don't have any idea who he is, do you?" I asked her with a smile.

"Not a clue," she said happily. "Why are we offended that he's here?"

"I'm not offended. I just didn't realize he was well off enough to eat dinner here. He must have saved more money than I thought." He'd shifted to a smaller bandage, but it was still pretty noticeable. That tree branch must have done a real number on him.

"Who are we talking about?" Lincoln asked.

"Jim Hicks," I said as I looked again in his direction.

"I understand that he's made a great deal of money as a real estate agent," Lincoln said. "I've handled a few closings for him, and I wouldn't be breaking too many rules if I said that he's extremely well off. How do you know him, Christy?"

"He wants to buy Memories and Dreams and run it himself," I explained. "He told me that he's growing tired of real estate."

"You understand that you don't have the authority to sell it, don't you?" Lincoln asked, clearly puzzled by the news. "Unless..."

"Unless what?" Marybeth asked, eager for a new tidbit.

"I'm sorry, but I'm not at liberty to discuss that with *you*," Lincoln said. "It's a matter of attorney-client privilege."

"I waive it," I said, and then I waved my hand in front of Lincoln's face. "See? This is me waiving."

"We both know those are two different words," Lincoln said.

"I'll waive whatever you'd like," I said. "I'm authorizing you to speak freely in front of Marybeth."

"I'm sure that she appreciates the gesture," Lincoln said

with a frown, "but I'd have to advise against it. Including a third party, your confidentiality with me would be in jeopardy."

"That's okay," Marybeth said as she stood. "I need to powder my nose, anyway."

I started to get up to join her when she put a hand on my shoulder. "You stay here, Christy. Otherwise my gesture will have been in vain."

After she left the table, I asked, "Was that strictly necessary? I'm going to tell her everything you say later, you know that, don't you?"

"What you choose to do after we talk is none of my business," he said.

"Well, what's the earth-shattering news now that we've gotten rid of Marybeth?"

"There's an option I haven't discussed with you yet. You seemed overwhelmed the last time we spoke, so I didn't want to put more on you than you could handle."

"I appreciate the thought, but you have to promise me that you'll never do that again. My father was overprotective to the point of smothering me, and I won't let any man treat me that way again. Do we understand each other?"

"Loud and clear," he said, obviously taken back a bit by my reaction.

"I'm sorry. I didn't mean anything by it. It's just that I've had enough men in my life trying to shield me than I care to think about."

"Understood," he said in a gentler tone. "Christy, you have an escape clause if you really want to exercise it," Lincoln said.

"What is it? Where do I have to sign?"

Lincoln looked at me cryptically before he spoke. "You'd honestly give it all up, just like that?"

"I guess that would depend on a few things. Would it mean that I'd have to give up *everything*?" I asked.

"It would mean exactly that, but remember, if you get out now, I should warn you that it would mean that Cora's cousins will get it all if you opt out early, and you'll be left with nothing. The penalty is rather harsh."

I thought about what it would mean to walk away from Cora's legacy. Could I do it, just sign my rights over to two women my boss and friend hadn't even liked? What would happen to the shop in their hands? They wouldn't run it. I knew that much just from what Cora had told me about them. No, they'd turn the sale over to a broker and get every last dime they could squeeze out of it. The basic premise of Memories and Dreams would die with Cora, and I couldn't stand the thought of it. Then I realized that I'd also be turning my back on something that desperately needed to be done. If I didn't have access to the shop, how would I ever solve what had happened to Cora and Midnight? "If it's all the same to you, I think I'll leave things the way they are right now."

"Good. I can't tell you how glad I am to hear that," I said.

"Is it safe for me to come back?" Marybeth asked from a distance. "If not, I can make another lap around the place."

"Come on," I said as I patted her chair seat. "We're all finished."

"With good results, I trust?" she asked.

I nodded, and Marybeth smiled. "Excellent. Now, tell me more about the real estate man. While you two were talking, he looked at you as though you were a pork chop still on the bone, Christy. You're not selling out to him, are you?"

"Not a chance," I said.

"Super. Hang on. He's coming over to our table."

I looked over to see Jim Hicks heading our way. Maybe, if we were lucky, he was just heading to the restroom.

No such luck. "Christy, it's good to see you getting out. I trust you've had some time to consider my proposal."

"She's not interested," Lincoln said.

"It's nice of you to speak for her, Counselor, but I'd rather hear it directly from her, if you don't mind," Jim Hicks said with a smile.

"That's entirely up to her, of course," Lincoln said, "but she couldn't sell you the space even if she wanted to. There are provisions in place barring it."

"As competent as I've heard that you are, I'm sure that we could work around any technicalities," the real estate agent said.

Lincoln smiled at him, but there was not the slightest hint of warmth in it. "You're free to try."

"Well?" Jim Hicks asked me. "What do you say, Christy? Are you game?"

"Thanks for the offer, but I've decided to stay where I am and honor Cora's last wishes," I said simply.

"Fair enough. I wish you nothing but the best, then."

"The man is persistent, I'll have to give him that," I said after Jim Hicks left the restaurant.

"Don't blame him. It's his nature not to take no for an answer," Lincoln said. "If he gives you any more trouble in spite of what he just said, let me know and I'll deal with him."

"I don't think he will, but if he does, I can handle things myself, as nice as your offer might be," I said.

"Understood," Lincoln said as he picked up one of the menus our waiter had stealthily put in front of each of us. "Now, what looks good?"

Marybeth and I exchanged glances, and then we shared smiles. It felt good being out among friends. Once again, her instincts had been dead on the money.

I was still trying to decide between the salmon and the steak when Marybeth's phone rang. As she started to answer, she said to us both, "I apologize, but my boss warned me that he might have to call tonight."

She stood as she said, "Hello," and moved toward the bar, talking animatedly with her employer as she walked.

"What was that all about?" Lincoln asked.

"I don't know. This is all news to me."

The waiter came over while Marybeth was still talking in

the bar on her phone. "Are we ready to order?"

"It will be another minute," I said. "Our friend had to take a phone call."

"Of course," he said and moved away, though he was clearly not pleased with Marybeth's absence. It appeared that our server didn't approve of cell phones, and I wasn't sure that I didn't agree with him.

I laughed. "He's not a fan of cell phones, is he?"

"Clearly. He's got a good point, though. I'm not all that fond of them myself," Lincoln replied. "I've been meaning to ask you. How was your day today?"

"Stressful," I said.

"Anything in particular that you'd care to talk about?"

I considered telling him about Cora's cryptic puzzles, but I wasn't sure it was something I should discuss with anyone else just yet. "No, not really," I said.

It was obvious that Lincoln was disappointed by my decision not to share with him, but I didn't know what else to do.

Marybeth came back to the table, and Lincoln started to stand. Say what you will about Southern men, but most of them had learned their manners at their mothers' knees. I never resisted the opportunity to have someone hold a door for me, or stand up in my presence. It made me feel special, and in the end, what exactly was so wrong with that? I'd had a few girlfriends from college who had come to North Carolina from up north, and they'd all been patently delighted by the unexpected show of respect and courtesy.

"Sit," she said as she hovered near the table. "I'm afraid that I'm going to have to bail out on you both. There's a new district manager, and my boss is doing her best to finish a handful of reports that should have been done months ago. She's volunteered me to help her, and I'm in no position to say no."

"We can always do this another night," I said as I started to get up.

"Are you kidding? I know how hard it was for you to

agree to do this tonight. There's no way I'm giving you a rain check. Besides, I've already called a taxi. Stay, and enjoy. I'll see you later, Christy."

Marybeth was gone before we could protest further, and Lincoln looked at me with a grin once she had left. "Is it just me, or have we just been set up?"

"There's no doubt in my mind," I said. "Marybeth thinks that we belong together. I didn't have any idea how proactive she'd be trying to make it happen, though. This is pretty transparent. Do you want to go?"

"Actually, I'm kind of hungry, and we both have to eat. Plus, if we indulge her this once, we can tell her that she's not allowed to do any more matchmaking between us. How does that sound to you?"

"Do you honestly think it will stop her?" I asked him. "You've known her longer than I have."

"That might be true, but there's no doubt in my mind that you know her much better now."

I thought about it, and then I said, "You're right. Well, truth be told, I'm kind of hungry myself. Let's go ahead and eat."

Our waiter approached. "Is there going to be another delay?"

"Actually, we're ready to order," I said. "It will just be the two of us after all."

"Excellent," he said.

After we both ordered, he left us to place our orders.

"Christy, I hope you realize that you can trust me with whatever is on your mind. As your attorney, anything you say to me will be kept confidential."

"It's not that I'm worried about you blabbing to anybody," I said. "I just don't want you to think that I'm an idiot."

"That would be impossible," he said.

I doubted that would be true, especially if I ever decided to mention my ghost cat to him. Still, he might be of some help to me. "How are you at puzzles?" I asked.

"Crossword or jigsaw?" he asked. "Not that it matters. I'm proud to say that I'm excellent at both varieties."

That was another thing that we had in common, but that hadn't been what I was talking about. "I was thinking more like word games."

Lincoln smiled broadly, and I could see how Marybeth had fallen for him in high school. He was decently good looking, but when he smiled, it was as though a light had been triggered inside, and he absolutely radiated. "Just try me," Lincoln said.

I pulled out the note I'd found in Cora's wooden box. "Let me read you something, and then you can tell me what you think."

I read the poem to him aloud, but I just about didn't need the physical reminder of what Cora had written, I'd read it so much lately.

The riches of the world are hidden away,
Masked in the Devil's Light.
A chest of fire burns deep within,
Hiding the heart of Midnight.

"Does that mean anything to you?" I asked.

"Where did you find it?" Lincoln asked as he reached for the poem. I didn't see any reason not to give it to him. After all, I'd just asked him to help.

"As a matter of fact, it was in the wooden box that I chose as one of my bequests from Cora."

"Then you knew this was there all along?" he asked as he waved it in the air. "I wondered why you'd choose something so commonplace."

Again, I couldn't exactly tell him that I'd picked the box because of my ghost cat, but I had to say *something*. "Like I said before, it has sentimental value," I said. "The note came as a surprise, but Cora was always leaving me puzzles and clues buried around the shop for me. It was a way to keep things interesting for both of us, and besides, I really got to know our inventory as I hunted for clues."

"The hidden riches of the world could refer to something

of great value, or on a more esoteric note, it could be referring to something less concrete, like love. The second line could be interpreted a number of ways. The devil's light. What an odd phrasing. Let's consider this for a moment. What color is most associated with the devil? It has to be red, wouldn't you agree? Tell me, are there any red lights anywhere in the shop?"

My astonished smile gave me away, because Lincoln quickly asked, "Christy, have you cracked any of it yet on your own?" he asked.

"Just that part, I swear. I must say, I'm impressed with your analytical skills, Counselor," I said, and it was the truth.

"As far as I'm concerned, it's just a natural offshoot of my profession," Lincoln said, but he was still clearly pleased with the compliment. "Tell me. What was the devil's light?"

"The emergency exit sign," I said. "When the shop was dark, the x in 'exit' was dark, so I figured that something was blocking the light, and I was right."

"X marks the spot," Lincoln said. "What did you find there?"

"Well, I uncovered a new clue, but I'm not sure what it means yet."

At that moment, our server appeared with our food.

"If it's okay with you, I'll show you later," I said.

"Now you're just teasing me," Lincoln answered with a grin. "But that's fine."

If the waiter heard Lincoln's comment, he chose not to acknowledge it.

The food was wonderful, but I worried at first that Lincoln would pester me for more information, but our conversation during dinner took an entirely different direction, one based more on laughter than solving clues. It was the nicest meal out I'd had in some time, and for a brief moment, Midnight's demise had left the forefront of my thoughts. I had to keep reminding myself that my pleasure wasn't being disloyal to my old friend. He'd want me to be happy.

I knew that as strongly as I knew my own name.

When the check came, Lincoln reached for it before I could even move.

"We should really split that," I said.

"Are you kidding? I offered to buy dinner and drinks for all three of us," he said with a smile. "The way I see it, I'm getting a break here. Should we get something to go for Marybeth?"

I shook my head and laughed. "No, this was her bright idea. She should have to pay for the privilege of meddling with our lives."

Lincoln nodded, but then he added, "You know that I'm interested in you, Christy, so I can't really join in your complaints about what she did. While it's true that Marybeth went about this the wrong way, I can't honestly say that I'm sorry that she did it."

His directness caught me off-guard. "Don't mince words, Lincoln. Tell me how you really feel."

He shrugged. "I say what's on my mind."

"I'm sorry, but I'm not in any position right now to reciprocate. Losing Cora and Midnight has clouded my emotions too much at the moment."

"I'm not pressing you for any kind of response," he said hastily. "I just wanted you to know how I felt."

"Well, I do, and I appreciate it."

Lincoln's smile returned. "Which one, my candidness, or my declaration of affection?"

"Both," I said. "Now, why don't you give me a ride back home so I can let my dear sweet roomie know that she's not allowed to meddle in our lives anymore."

"Do you honestly think it will do any good?" Lincoln asked as he left the money for the check and a healthy tip as well.

"Probably not, but the words still need to be spoken," I said. "Thank you most kindly for dinner, kind sir. It was delicious."

"You're most welcome. I should be the one thanking

you. I can't remember having so much fun out."

As he held the car door open for me, I slid onto the seat as I thanked him.

Lincoln headed toward my place, and after a few minutes, he said, "You never told me what the next clue you found was."

"I shouldn't have dragged you into a game that Cora and I liked to play."

"Are you kidding? I'm really enjoying myself," he said. "Christy, you can't leave me hanging like this. What did you find behind that sign?"

I smiled at him, and I knew that Lincoln hadn't just been trying to placate me before. He was genuinely interested in the puzzle for the puzzle itself.

"It was a playing card, and a dried frond from a fern."

Lincoln nodded. "Which card was it?"

"The Ace of Diamonds," I said.

Lincoln pondered this as he drove a few more miles, and then asked me an interesting question, something I hadn't considered. "In what order were they when you removed them? Do you remember?"

"The fern frond was in front of the playing card. If it helps, it was dried out and crumbling at my touch, so the idea of identifying it isn't going to work."

"That's okay. I don't think I'm going to need to see it," he said with a deep smile.

"Do you know what it means?" I asked. This man was quick!

"I have a hunch. Do you have to get straight home, or can we detour by your shop? I know it's late, and you've spent all day there, but I doubt that I'll be able to get to sleep not knowing if I'm right or not."

"Go to Memories and Dreams, then, by all means," I said.

"Are we rhyming now, or should I stop and take a bow?" he asked with a grin.

"It was inadvertent," I said. "I've got enough tasks right now without worrying about rhyming my lines."

"Perhaps for another day," he said. "How do you feel about puns?"

Most of the people I knew who were fascinated with words adored them, and I was no exception. "I always say, the louder the groan, the better the pun," I said.

"Seconded," he replied. "It's good to find a kindred spirit."

"I know exactly what you mean."

We were still two blocks from the shop when I noticed a dark figure standing near the front door trying to peer in.

"Lincoln, someone's trying to break in again," I said. "Call the police."

Chapter 10

"I can do better than that," Lincoln said as he put the accelerator down and flashed on his high beams. "You call the police, and I'll try to see who's got trouble on their mind tonight."

As we raced toward my storefront, the figure ran away, ducking between two buildings before I could catch a glimpse of whoever had just been there.

"They're gone," I said.

"You should still call the police," Lincoln replied. "Christy, I shouldn't have gotten so carried away. I'm sorry if I scared the burglar off."

"I'm not," I replied. "I've already been broken into once this week, and I'm in no mood to repeat the experience," I said as I dialed Sheriff Adam Kent's telephone number.

"What's wrong now?" the sheriff asked as he picked up on the other end.

"What makes you think something is wrong?" I asked.

"Christy, you wouldn't be calling me if it weren't."

"Somebody just tried to break into Memories and Dreams again," I said.

"You should have started the conversation with that particular little tidbit. I'll be there in two minutes."

I started to tell him that there wasn't any hurry since whoever had been at the door had taken off, but I never got a chance to say another word.

"Can you believe that? He hung up on me," I told Lincoln.

"Is he coming?"

"On a dead run, if the way he signed off is any indication," I answered. "Should we wait for him inside the shop?"

"It might be a better idea if we wait in the car," Lincoln said.

"Okay, I'm game if you are." Two minutes later, the

sheriff showed up in his patrol car.

"Where's the suspect?" he asked after he pulled up beside us.

"He took off between those two buildings," Lincoln said as he pointed to the spot where our would-be burglar ran.

"You didn't try to follow him, did you?" the sheriff asked.

"No, once we scared him away from the building, we figured that it was your job to track him down," I said.

"That's smart thinking. Stay in the car, both of you," the sheriff said as he pulled out his revolver and followed the bad guy's footsteps. "I'll be back soon."

"Shouldn't you be calling for backup or something?" I asked as he started to vanish between the buildings.

"Don't worry. I can handle this by myself," he said.

"I don't like this," I said after the sheriff had been gone a few minutes. "What if the burglar's waiting to ambush him?"

"I don't think the sheriff has anything to worry about. Whoever it was has to be long gone by now. Besides, I've known that man for years. He's perfectly capable of protecting himself; there's no doubt in my mind."

I hadn't realized that I was holding my breath until the sheriff came back around the building and walked toward us. I was happy to see that his gun was now reholstered. "Did you see anybody?" I asked as we got out.

"Not a soul," he said. "Thanks for staying put, though."

"You're welcome," Lincoln said as he smiled at me.

The sheriff double-checked the front door as we all walked over to it. "It's still locked up tight. The back is okay, too. That was fast, getting an alarm system installed. Good job."

"I had the feeling at the time that I was locking the barn door after the horses got out, but it turns out that it was a pretty good idea after all."

"Who did the installation for you?" the sheriff asked me.

I gave him Emily's name, and he nodded in approval.

"She does good work. Listen, don't hesitate to call if you see anything else suspicious around here."

He started to get back into his car when Lincoln called out, "Sheriff, Christy would probably sleep better tonight if you doubled up your patrols around here."

"It's already been taken care of," he said, arching an eyebrow at Lincoln as he spoke. "You two have a good night, at least what's left of it."

After Sheriff Kent was gone, I said, "I'm not sure that the sheriff approves of us being out this late without a chaperone."

"He can go bark at the moon if he doesn't like it. As for me, I'm having the time of my life. How about you?"

"I'll say this for you, Lincoln. You're not a bland first date."

"Is that what this is? I would never have allowed Marybeth to tag along if I'd known it was going to turn into that." Then he flashed that smile at me again. At least I caught myself before I returned it in full force.

"You know what I mean. Should we call it a night?"

"If you insist," he said, clearly disappointed by my suggestion. "But what I'd really like to do is go inside the shop and see if my hunch is right."

I'd nearly forgotten about his awaiting clue interpretation in all of the excitement. "I'm happy to go in if you are. Don't you have to get up early tomorrow, though? I don't have to open the shop until ten, so I can always sleep in tomorrow."

"I'm willing to sacrifice a little sleep in order to do some digging," he said. I was starting to feel as though Lincoln was my kind of guy, though I wasn't about to tell *him* that.

I unlocked the front door, and then I stepped aside. "Lead on. After all, this is your party tonight."

"I'd be delighted," he said as he walked into the darkened shop. I flipped on a few lights, but not all of them. I didn't want anyone to think for one second that I was actually open for business at this time of night.

I locked the door behind us, and then I asked Lincoln, "What do we do now?"

"We need to go straight to the back," he said. "If I'm right, we'll know it soon enough."

"Do you want to see the playing card and whatever is left of that fern frond first?" I asked.

"No, if my hunch is right, we won't need either one of them."

"And if you're wrong?" I asked as I followed him into the back.

"Then I still get to spend a little more time with you, so in a way, it's a win-win situation, don't you think?"

"I reserve judgment until I see where this is headed," I said, though I smiled slightly in spite of my austere comment. Lincoln was fun to be with, I was just beginning to realize. I hoped that Midnight forgave me for acting like a high school girl, but I had a hunch that he would understand.

"Let me ask you one question before we go exploring. Is your heat not working, by any chance?"

"No, it's been down for a month," I said. "How could you possibly know that?"

He just smiled. "Follow me."

"Watch the boxes," I said as I opened the door, and he nimbly skipped through. I settled them back in place temporarily and followed him into the storeroom.

We walked over to the furnace together and he knelt down beside the access panel, but before Lincoln started to remove it, I put a hand on his. "I think you've been cryptic for long enough. What makes you think there's another clue hiding in there?"

"I just put two and two together," he said, "and if we find something interesting inside here, it will most emphatically add up to four."

"Explain."

He nodded, and his hands dropped from the screws that held the main furnace panel in place. "You said that Cora liked to share puzzles with you. You found two objects in the exit sign, a fern frond and a playing card. The value of the card is crucial in the clue."

"Fern plus Ace equals Furnace," I said as I finally got it. How had I missed that before? "I am an idiot."

"Losing Midnight has temporarily deadened your abilities. There's no shame in grieving for a lost friend," he said.

"I still should have caught that one. Would you mind stepping aside? I'd like to see exactly what Cora hid in our disabled furnace for myself."

Lincoln got up graciously, and I knelt down in his place. The screws had elongated ridges, and besides, they were already a bit loose, but it was still a bit of a task backing them out with my fingertips. Once the panel came off in my hands, I passed it over to Lincoln and then I peered inside.

It was too dark to see anything at first, and the last line of Cora's poem struck me.

It did indeed appear to be housing the heart of Midnight.

I reached over and grabbed a flashlight that Cora kept nearby for emergencies, and after I turned it on, I peered into the gloom.

What I found there made me wonder if I was seeing things.

It was a paper mache black cat, and someone, most likely Cora, had hand painted a collar and tag for it.

It said proudly 'Midnight,' and I wondered what my friend had been up to.

"So, that's it?" I asked as I looked at the cat in disbelief. "It was one of *those* puzzles."

"What do you mean?" Lincoln asked.

I put the cat down on the nearest table and explained, "Every now and then, Cora liked to have a little fun with me. She would build a treasure hunt into something outlandish and overblown, and then the prize would be something nearly worthless. I had my hopes up based on the clues she left me, but honestly, I can't blame her. She had no idea that someone was going to break into her shop and kill her before I could solve the puzzle."

"So, where does that leave you?" Lincoln asked.

"Well, for one thing, it's going to give me more time to focus on figuring out who killed Cora and Midnight. When I get that worked out, I'll know what whoever did it was looking for." I considered telling him right then and there about Cora's notebook, but I wasn't sure that I was ready to besmirch her name quite yet. If I could find it myself, I could check it out and then destroy it if that's what it called for, so no one would ever be faced with anything Cora had speculated about them. I'd have to take time to think about sharing the information with anyone else, but not tonight, not while I was standing so close to where Cora and Midnight had died. I could tell Lincoln about it, but then I'd never be able to take it back. I had to be sure of my decision when I made it.

"Do you think the murder was tied into the burglary attempts?" Lincoln asked.

"Don't you?" I asked him in a roundabout way. I was avoiding his glance, and I had a hunch that he knew it.

"I do," he replied. "I just wish we knew what there was so valuable."

"Whatever it is, we're not going to find it in the storeroom," I answered.

"What makes you think that?" he asked.

"Well, in the first two burglaries where the burglar actually gained access inside, the messes were restricted to the sales floor. That makes me believe that whoever broke in had reason to believe that whatever they wanted was somewhere on display, but I've already looked everywhere, and I couldn't find a thing."

"Maybe you just need another set of fresh eyes," he said.

"Maybe," I said as evasively as I could manage.

"There's something else that's been troubling me," Lincoln said after a brief pause. "If there was something here *that* valuable and Cora didn't realize it, why didn't the thief just buy it and be done with it?"

"I have a couple of theories about that," I said.

"I'd love to hear them."

"First, what if there's something that ties them to the item that they don't want known about them?"

"I'd love an example, if you can come up with one," he said.

"It could have already been stolen from someone else when Cora bought it, and by buying it, the thief could be connected to some link that they wanted to stay hidden."

"Does that happen very often?" Lincoln asked.

"What's that?"

"Are you in the habit of buying many stolen items at the shop?"

"We never fenced anything for anyone, at least not on purpose," I said. "And we certainly never made it a habit of buying stolen goods. Then again, not many folks come in with a receipt from their original purchase, so who's to say? Cora had pretty good radar about things like that. I suppose that's just one more skill I'm going to have to develop if I stay on and eventually take over the business."

"I hope you do," Lincoln said as he moved a little closer to me. Was this man seriously about to try to kiss me in my own storeroom? I was still deciding on how I was going to react when the chance slipped past me.

There was a pounding on the front door, and the mood was broken. It had nearly happened, though, and I still wasn't sure if I'd wanted it to or not.

"Let's go see who that is," I said.

Lincoln surprised me by smiling. "To be continued," he said with a grin.

Now what had he meant by that? I supposed that only time would tell, but I had to admit, I was interested in finding out.

"Celeste, what are you doing here at this time of night?" I asked the café owner as I opened the door for her. I'd grabbed the paper mache cat almost as an afterthought, thinking that Marybeth might get a kick out of it.

Celeste glanced at it, but she didn't comment. "I was doing inventory at the café when I spotted the light on in back of your shop. If you hadn't come to the door, I was going to call the sheriff."

"Thanks," I said. "It's nice to have a neighborhood watch here."

She looked a little guilty as she nodded. "That's sort of what I was hoping to talk to you about."

Lincoln got the hint immediately. "Christy, I'll wait for you in the car. Take your time, I'm sure I have a ton of messages waiting on my voice mail."

"We won't be long," Celeste said. As she watched him walk back to her car, she added, "I always liked him."

"That's nice," I said. "Celeste, what's so important that it won't wait until morning?"

"I said something to you today that I instantly regretted. I was out of line, and I need to apologize for it if I have any prayer of getting to sleep tonight."

I tried to remember everything that she'd said to me recently, but I wasn't able to come up with anything out of the ordinary. "I'm sorry, but I honestly don't have any idea what you're talking about."

"My comment about buying this place so I could expand was in the worst taste possible, especially after what you've been through recently. It wasn't like me. I'm not a woman who pushes and pushes until she gets what she wants, and it's important for me to know that you realize it, too. I didn't think about what I was saying when we chatted. Can you find it in your heart to forgive me?"

I saw the troubled expression on her face, and on a whim, I stepped forward and hugged her. "There's nothing to forgive," I said.

I could feel the tenseness leave her body as I said it, and I knew that it really *had* been troubling her.

"Are you really going to make it that easy on me?" she asked with a smile as we broke our hug. "Christy, you could make me jump through a few hoops first, you know. I figure that I deserve at least that."

"Friends don't do that to each other," I said.

Celeste studied me for a second, and then she smiled. "We *are* friends, aren't we?"

"I'd like to think so," I said. "Listen, I'm glad we cleared that up, but I don't like leaving Lincoln waiting for me."

"I understand completely. Thank you so much, Christy. You've made me really happy today."

"I'm glad I could help," I said.

"I can be a very powerful ally," Christy said. "You wouldn't believe the variety of folks who eat at my café. If you need anything, and I mean anything, don't hesitate to ask me. Would you promise me that?"

"I might just take you up on it," I said, suddenly realizing how Celeste might be able to get me information that no one else could.

"I'll be upset if you don't. Now, go to your young man, and I'll see you in the morning."

"He's not exactly my young man," I said.

"Don't bet on it. I saw the way Lincoln was looking at you. I'm not afraid to admit that I'm jealous. It's been too long since someone looked at me the same way."

I rejoined Lincoln, and as I got in, he asked, "What was that all about?"

"She told me earlier that she wouldn't mind buying the shop so she could expand the café, and after I left, evidently she started feeling guilty about the offer."

"So you forgave her," Lincoln said with the hint of a grin.

"I did. She was sweet about it, so I decided to let her off easy."

"Good for you," Lincoln said. "Where to now?"

"Would you mind taking me home? I have another big day tomorrow. I'm planning on getting to the shop as soon as I can and try to discover what I've missed so far."

He looked at me and asked me softly, "Would you like some help? I'm not due in court until ten tomorrow morning, but I'd be delighted to help as long as I can."

I laughed. "Thanks for the offer, but people will talk."

"Let them," he said. "I don't mind if you don't. What time are we going to get started?"

"I was thinking about seven," I said.

Lincoln laughed slightly in surprise, and then he grinned. "Seven it is."

"Do you mind if I recruit Marybeth, too?" I asked.

"Why would I mind that?" he asked, but he was clearly disappointed that we wouldn't be hunting alone. "The more the merrier, right?"

"Right," I said. Until I could figure out how I felt about Lincoln, it might be wise not to be alone with him. Losing Midnight and Cora so recently, my heart wasn't ready to open up to anybody just yet.

I just hoped that someday it would, and that Lincoln would still be around and interested.

But I wasn't betting on it.

It could just be that our timing was off.

That was the story of my love life over the past few years, but it was something I could deal with. I had to. Until the person who had taken Midnight and Cora from me was brought to justice, there wasn't much room in my heart for someone new.

Chapter 11

"What was that all about?" Marybeth asked me as I walked into the house after Lincoln dropped me off.

"I'm sure I don't know what you're talking about. How was your meeting?" I asked with a smile.

"We both know that I didn't have one. I saw that little move in the car. You barely kissed his cheek before you got out, Christy. You're not going to catch him that way."

"Who said I wanted to catch anybody?" I asked. "Were you spying on me?"

"You bet I was. I was just hoping for something a little more R-rated than that. I would have even settled for PG-13, but instead, all I got was G."

"You need to get a life of your own," I said as I picked up a throw pillow, laughed, and then threw it at her.

"If you keep this up, I just might have to. Seriously, how was dinner? Were there any sparks? And what's that wretched thing that you're holding?"

I passed over my new paper mache cat. "This was the grand prize at the end of Cora's big treasure hunt," I said.

"Some prize," Marybeth replied, and then she put it down on the coffee table. I wondered what Midnight would make of it, if he ever came back. I was living in constant fear now that the last time I saw him would truly *be* the last time, but I knew that I couldn't go on living that way. Whether he decided to stay or to go, I knew that there was nothing *I* could do about it. I'd keep on my course and hope that Midnight's next clue led to something more valuable than a craft project. Was that why he'd led me to it, so I could discover his likeness hiding in the furnace? I knew that cats could be vain, but that was stretching things a bit even for my taste. "When are you going to see Lincoln again?" Marybeth asked. "Please tell me that you at least made another date with the man."

"We're getting together tomorrow morning, as a matter

of fact."

"Wow, that was fast," Marybeth said with a grin.

"It's not like that. I've decided to dig deeper into what might be so valuable in the shop that someone would risk breaking into it so many times."

"How many times has it happened? What are you talking about?" Marybeth asked after she saw that I wasn't kidding.

"That's right, you haven't heard yet. I was going to show Lincoln something I found at the shop today, but when we got there, someone was trying to break in."

"I thought Emily put a new security system in for you," Marybeth said.

"That was probably what slowed them down," I answered. "Remind me to thank Emily for doing that installation so quickly. Who knows what would have happened otherwise. Anyway, I told Lincoln that you'd be joining us in the morning. Please tell me that you're going to be able to give me an hour or two of your time."

"Do you *really* want me there?" she asked, all kidding aside for the moment.

"I do," I said solemnly.

"Then, I'll be there," Marybeth said reassuringly. "Don't worry, Christy. Whatever it is, we'll find it."

"I hope so," I said. "With this killer on the loose, I'm as jumpy as I've ever been in my life. I'm afraid of what might be around every corner. I'm like a scared little kid, aren't I?"

"Actually, I think you're just being prudent," Marybeth said soberly. "It sounds as though you've got every reason to be worried about your personal safety."

"Hey, I was hoping for a little reassurance here," I said.

"Everything's going to work out just fine in the end," she said with a smile that was clearly forced.

Her lack of sincerity was rather alarming.

Marybeth stood, and then she petted the paper mache cat. "If we're getting up early tomorrow, might I suggest we turn in early tonight?"

"That's a brilliant idea," I said.

"Don't look so surprised. I get them every now and then."

I stopped her and hugged her. "Thank you."

"For what?" she asked, clearly startled by my gesture.

"Just for being you," I said.

"In that case, it's my pleasure," she replied.

I waited as long as I could for Midnight to reappear, but in the end, it was just Shadow who joined me in my bed.

I went to sleep dreaming that the nightmare that had happened to my cat and my boss was nothing more than that, but there was always a part of me that knew that it was all too real.

"Coffee?" I asked Marybeth brightly the next morning as she dragged herself into the kitchen at a time that was way too early for her.

"Christine, no one on earth has any right to be as perky as you are in the morning," she said as she greedily took the full cup of coffee from me that I had ready and waiting for her.

"I can't help it," I said with a smile. "You know me. I wake up this way every day."

"Don't remind me. When do we have to be at the shop?"

I glanced at the clock on the oven. "We've still got half an hour," I said.

"I'd better take my coffee with me, then," she said as she started for the shower.

I was glad that I'd already taken mine. Though we each had our own bathroom, the hot water supply in our old house was limited. Hopefully I'd taken mine early enough to give the boiler a chance to build its reserves back up a little.

To my surprise, Marybeth came downstairs ten minutes before we needed to be at the shop. I was caught off-guard even more when I saw that she was wearing an old flannel shirt and blue jeans. "Are you seriously going to work like that?"

"I'm not about to go digging around in your shop in one of my suits," she said. "I'll come home later and take another shower before I go to work."

"I really appreciate you helping me like this. You know that, don't you?"

"I'd do anything for you, and if this doesn't prove it, nothing will," Marybeth said with a smile. "Now, let's get started."

Lincoln was already waiting for us when we got to Memories and Dreams. Unlike Marybeth, he'd chosen to wear his work clothes, which for him meant a nice three-piece suit. "You're going to get dirty," Marybeth said when she saw him.

"I'll manage somehow," he said. Lincoln held up a box and a bag. "I stopped to get donuts and coffee on the way. I hope that's all right."

"It's perfect," I said. "Thank you."

Marybeth grabbed one of the coffees, despite her travel mug clenched tightly in one hand. "Hey, you've already got one," I said.

"I thought you knew me better than that, Christy. I can *never* have too much coffee." She smiled at Lincoln. "Thanks for thinking of us."

"My pleasure," he said. "Shall we go in and get started?"

"I'm ready if you two are," I said. I'd debated the night before about telling them to be on the lookout for Cora's notebook, and I finally decided in the wee hours that it was important information that I couldn't keep from them any longer. "If either one of you find a black and white composition notebook, I need to see it immediately. It's exactly like the ones we used to use in school."

"What's in it?" Marybeth asked. "Is it full of Cora's dirty little secrets?"

"I don't know. An inventory of the store's contents would be nice," Lincoln said.

"Sorry, but Marybeth is closer. It turns out that Cora kept a notebook full of speculations concerning the citizens of this town, and it's missing."

"Surely you don't think that was the cause of the murder,

do you?" Lincoln asked.

"If your name were in there, and it revealed a secret that you thought was safe, wouldn't you do whatever it took to get your hands on that notebook?" I asked.

"If I were a bad guy, you mean," Lincoln said. "There aren't any skeletons in *my* closet."

"I'm not accusing you of anything. I'm just saying that it could have given someone incentive enough to get rid of Cora if what was written in there was bad enough." Wow, my supposition sounded kind of weak once I said it out loud. Then again, there was no telling what someone might do to protect a secret they wanted to stay hidden.

"Can I glance through it if I find it first?" Marybeth asked devilishly. "It must make for some fascinating reading."

"We probably need to read it if we're going to find the killer, but I was hoping that we wouldn't take much joy out of it."

"Christy, you don't have to worry. I won't spread any rumors about what we find," Marybeth said. "That's the *most* I'm going to be able to promise, though."

"How about you, Counselor?" I asked Lincoln.

"It might not hurt to know who we're dealing with here," he said calmly.

"Fine, we'll all read it, but in order to do that, we'll have to find it first, so good luck, everyone."

"Wow, I've *never* seen such an eclectic collection of *stuff* in my life," Lincoln said after we'd been sifting through the items in the shop for two hours. We still had one more hour to go, but so far, we hadn't found a single thing that warranted the attention the shop had gotten lately, including Cora's missing notebook.

"Call it whatever you'd like," Marybeth said, "but to me, it's just one big indoor flea market, and I've got the fleas to prove it."

"Oh, we're a few notches better than *that*," I said, defending my shop. "We just cater to the more unique individuals who happen to pass through our doors."

"Unique?" she asked with a laugh. "Is that what they're calling them these days?"

I refused to be baited, and just smiled at her. "Back to work, you two. We don't have much time left, and I'm worried that if we don't find something important soon, we might not get a second chance."

"Yes, ma'am," Marybeth said with a smile.

After awhile, I began to believe that this was hopeless. The store had so many nooks and crannies, it was nearly impossible to find something that a determined robber might possibly want.

As I searched, I decided to at least organize things a little better. Grabbing a hardback from the jewelry section, I carried it over to the book section, a hodgepodge of fiction and nonfiction we kept on hand for our benefit as much as our customers. Cora never minded if I found something to take home, as long as I returned it, and I knew that she did the same. Honestly, who would ever want the volume in my hands, anyway? *Secrets of the Ages* was supposed to be about the world's greatest conspiracy theories, but it had been published in the 50s, and there was no doubt that whatever outlandish theories it contained had been rehashed dozens of times.

The thing is, the second I picked it up, I knew that something was wrong with it.

Books have a certain heft to them, and this one was lacking the mass of what I'd expected. Cracking the cover open, I was surprised to find that most of the pages had been hollowed out with a razor.

But instead of jewels or money, what I found there was equally as interesting.

It was Cora's black and white notebook, neatly tucked away as the perfect purloined letter, her theories hidden safely away in someone else's.

"Look at this," I said loudly.

Marybeth and Lincoln joined me quickly.

"What did you find?" Lincoln asked me.

"It's Cora's journal," I said.

Lincoln looked a little deflated. "I was hoping for something a shade more valuable."

"Are you nuts?" Marybeth asked as she snatched it from my hands. "This could very well be the reason that Cora and Midnight were both murdered."

"Over some random scribbling in a book?" he asked.

"It makes perfect sense to me," I said. "Secrets can be powerful motivators."

Lincoln shrugged. "I'm not denying that. I just wonder how many of Cora's ramblings are based on anything factual."

"There's only one way to find out," Marybeth said with delight. It was clear that she was really going to enjoy this. "Who's first on Cora's hit list?"

"Hey, I should be the one to read it first," I said. "After all, I'm the one who found it."

Marybeth nodded. "Do you know what? You are absolutely right. Here you go."

As I took the notebook from her, I suddenly wasn't so sure that I wanted to read it. I'd liked Cora an awful lot, and I didn't want the things she'd written in her notebook to change my mind about her. Then again, if it helped me find her killer, I was just going to have to swallow my distaste and do it.

I opened the book carefully and started to examine it.

"What's it say?" Marybeth asked impatiently. "Is it anything good?"

"I'm not sure," I answered. "It's not exactly indexed. There are names, and they are accompanied by random observations and theories attached to them."

Lincoln said, "I'm glad you had some success in your hunt, but I need to go now."

"You don't approve of this, do you?" I asked him as I closed the notebook again. Suddenly, Lincoln's opinion mattered to me.

"I completely understand why you have to do this," he said. "I just need to go prepare for court."

"You didn't answer my question," I said.

He smiled at me. "I'm a lawyer, remember? It's what we do."

"I mean it," I said. "I want to know how you feel about this."

He nodded, and his smile disappeared. "I suppose I just don't want my attitude about these people tainted by what you're about to read. Trust me, there are times *I* wish I knew quite a bit less about the people in our fair little town."

"It can't be helped, though," I said. "You just admitted that much."

"If you're not going to read it, at least let me have it," Marybeth said as she made a grab for the book.

"No, I'll do it," I said, "but I want to let Lincoln out before I get started."

The two of us walked the attorney to the front, and after I unlocked the door, he asked, "Would it be possible to have a late lunch with you? I really would like to know what you find in there."

"Sure, we'd love to go with you," Marybeth said. "What time would you like to pick us up?" She watched the expressions on our faces, and then she started laughing. "Relax you two. I know I wasn't included in that invitation."

"You know that you're welcome to join us," Lincoln said. "In fact, I insist."

"Nice try, but I'm going to let you off the hook. I have to be in Lincolnton and Gastonia all day, so I won't be available."

"Nevertheless, if your plans change, the invitation stands."

After he was gone, I smiled at Marybeth. "You really *love* doing that, don't you?"

"I don't know what you mean," she said with her wickedest grin.

"I'm sure that you don't," I said, matching it with one of

my own. "Let's go back and see what Cora had to say about our dear townsfolk."

Thirty minutes later, I was beginning to wonder if I should have taken Lincoln's advice after all. I'd read Cora's entries aloud, and Marybeth and I took turns being surprised by the things my former boss had written there.

"Let me see if I've got this straight," Marybeth said as I closed the book. "We've read things inflammatory enough to make a dozen people want to kill Cora to keep her from spreading rumors about them in that little notebook."

"Not a dozen," I said defensively. "Some of her claims weren't all that bad."

"Like Eugenia Coffee lacing her sodas with vodka every morning?" she asked.

"That's as good an example as any," I said. "I suspected as much about her, anyway."

"Sure, but seeing it written down like that is another thing entirely. Okay, I concede that not all of the things she said were worthy of homicide, but a few of them sure were."

"Let's try starting a suspect list, and add what Cora wrote about them," I said. "I know that it might not be complete, but it's as good a place to start as any."

"Agreed," Marybeth said as she looked around the back of the shop. "Is there anything here we can write on? I'm not sure I can keep everything straight unless we record it."

"How about this?" I asked as I got a portable chalkboard and stand from behind some boxes. "We use this whenever we have a sidewalk sale."

"That'll do just fine. Do you happen to have any white chalk on you?"

I dug around, but finally I said, "All I could come up with is this." It was purple, and the only reason that the piece I had was as large as it was was because it didn't show up all that well on the chalkboard.

"It'll be fine," she said. "Okay, let's start with names. You call them out, and I'll write them down."

I thumbed through the notebook, calling out names as I came across them. When I finished, we had Kelly Madigan, Jim Hicks, Professor Jenkins, Celeste from next door, Mayor Kelly, and Barbara Hastings listed on the board.

"I hate that Celeste's name is on here," I said. "I really like her."

"So do I, but we can't take her name off just because we enjoy eating her French toast," Marybeth said.

"I know you're right, but I still don't like it. Okay, now that we have the names, let's add their motives."

"That sounds good," Marybeth said as she started jotting down brief notes about each of our suspects. I thought her comment section was a little simplistic, but it did give us a general idea about where to look. According to Cora's notes, Kelly Madigan was a kleptomaniac who had escalated her thefts recently, Jim Hicks had cheated his former partner out of hundreds of thousands of dollars, Professor Jenkins was a fraud ripe for exposure, Celeste had done something mysterious and bad to her late husband, Mayor Kelly was having an affair with his next door neighbor, and Barbara Hastings was responsible for embezzling thousands of dollars from the school PTA.

I studied the list. "Wow, we live in a hotbed of crime, don't we? I didn't have a clue about any of this."

"Remember, we haven't confirmed *any* of this yet," Marybeth said. "As far as we know, *none* of this is true."

"If it weren't, why would Cora write it all down?" I asked.

"Who knows? Maybe she was trying her hand at writing a mystery, and she was going to base it on people she knew."

"Do you think she'd actually use their real names? I'm sure that she could get sued for that."

"The names would have been easy enough to change at the last second," Marybeth said, "but I think it would work just fine in a first draft. For someone not used to writing fiction, wouldn't it be easier just to base her writing on people she knew, and then change all of the names later?"

"I don't know," I said. "Cora never said anything about ever wanting to try her hand at writing."

"Okay, maybe this was just a way to amuse herself. I'm not saying that any of it means anything, but don't you think we owe it to her to try to figure out if any of these folks might have found out about her journal, and wanted to kill her to protect their secrets?"

"I can't think of any other reason for what's been happening. We've never had all that much of value in our shop. Well, except for this," I said as I pulled my necklace chain out from under my shirt. "Evidently *this* is worth more than I realized." I grabbed the chalk from Cora and added one more name to her list, David Whitman.

"He's broke and desperate, according to Cora," Marybeth said. "Is that motive enough for murder?"

"What you don't know is that his mother sold this without his blessing. Evidently it's worth a great deal more than the hundred dollars Cora paid for it, and David was pretty desperate to get it back."

"So, we have seven names on our list. It's kind of daunting, isn't it?" Marybeth asked.

"I'm sorry to say that I have a few more to add. We can't overlook the obvious. Cora's cousins, Sandy and Mandy, have the most to gain by her death. I'm certain they were under the impression that they were inheriting the shop. They had a real monetary stake in things."

"Should we go ahead and add their attorney, too?" Marybeth asked. "After all, the more the merrier."

"I'm hesitant to list him, since he wasn't mentioned in Cora's book, and he has no real motive to want her dead."

"Well, that's a relief. For a second there, I thought we might have to just add the entire telephone book for Noble Point. I'm not afraid to say that all of this overwhelms me."

"I'd feel the exact same way if we didn't have a secret weapon of our own," I replied.

"What are you talking about?"

"I've got an idea. Why don't we go ask our favorite

librarian and researcher to help us with our list?" I suggested. "If anybody in town knows about the folks written here, it's got to be Trudy."

Marybeth glanced at her watch. "I hate to do this, especially when it's just getting so interesting, but I've got those appointments, and I still have to go home, shower, and change before I go. Tell me what she says, though, okay?"

"I promise," I said, and I let her out of the shop. I had time to go next door for a quick cup of coffee before I had to open, but after what I'd just read about Celeste, I was in no hurry to see her. Lincoln had been right. Reading Cora's notebook had changed the way I looked at my friends in town, and I wasn't sure that I'd ever be able to look at any of them the same way again. The sooner I separated rumor and speculation from truth, the better. I took a quick photo of our list with my phone, locked the door behind me, and went off in search of Trudy.

Hopefully she'd be able to clear up some of the many questions I had about the people who surrounded me every day. I just wished that I had a new scarf to take her. I was asking an awful lot of her, but I honestly didn't know where else to turn.

Chapter 12

"Hey, Trudy. I hope you've got a little time, because I need some help," I said as I walked into the library where my friend worked. Trudy Jefferson had her nose in a book, which was no real surprise.

"Sure thing," she said as she marked her place with a bookmark designed from a winning entry in the last contest they'd held for their young readers. It was a bright green caterpillar, and the words, "Words Are Tasty" were emblazoned on it. "What can I do?" She tapped a few keys on her computer, and then she added, "I can access information from around the world right here. It's all pretty amazing, actually."

"This isn't as much library business as it is personal," I said.

She nodded. "I'm sorry, then. I can't help you until I'm on my break. It's library policy. You understand, don't you?"

"Of course," I said. It was too bad I'd lost my main research resource, but Trudy had to do her job before she could help me.

As I started back out of the library, she asked, "Where are you going, Christy?"

"I didn't think you could help me," I said.

"You never asked me when my break was," Trudy said with a grin as she looked at her watch. "In four, three, two, one. Okay, I'm on break."

"Excellent," I said. I looked around the room, and I knew that just because I couldn't see anyone didn't mean that they weren't there. "Is there somewhere we can go and talk in private? This is some pretty potentially volatile stuff."

Trudy frowned. "I'm supposed to have a volunteer from our Friends of the Library program, but she's late. Tell you what. Why don't you start talking, and if we get any company, we can postpone the rest of our conversation until we have a chance to chat. I'm sorry. I know that it's not ideal, but I'm afraid that it's the best I'm going to be able to do right now."

"I'll take what I can get," I said. "The thing is, it's critical that what we discuss is just between the two of us. You'll know more once I explain, but I need your solemn vow that you won't breathe a word of what I'm doing to anyone else."

"Done," she said.

"Is it honestly going to be that easy?" I asked her. "I figured you'd need something more than that."

"I realize that we haven't known each other a long time, but I can usually trust my instincts when it comes to knowing whether I can trust someone or not. I trust you. Is that foolish on my part?"

"No, I'd give myself a ringing endorsement if I could, though I would have no idea why you'd take my word for it."

"Christy, let's just start off trusting each other and go from there. What can I do for you?"

"I told you the truth when I said that I needed information. I'm just not sure how much of it you'll be able to get from your computer."

"You might be amazed. Now talk. We don't really know how much time we have."

"Okay, here goes. Cora kept a notebook, a journal really, and she said some pretty inflammatory things in it about the folks of Noble Point."

Trudy frowned. "I was wondering if it had turned up yet."

"You knew about Cora's hobby?" I asked.

"I knew of it," she said. "Is it as bad as some people around here think?"

"It's pretty harsh in places," I said. "I'm trying to use it to figure out who killed her and my Midnight," I said. "If she had information that could be damaging to someone, they might have killed her to keep her from telling anyone."

"It sounds like a reasonable assumption," Trudy said. "That might explain all of the break-ins you've been having, too."

"How do you know about those?"

"It's a small town, and besides, I keep a police scanner on by my bed. What can I say, it makes me feel safe knowing that the sheriff and his staff are out there working through the night. It must sound odd to you, though."

"If it helps you sleep, I'd say go for it," I said.

"Have you managed to narrow your list down at all?" she asked.

I opened my phone and pulled up the picture I'd taken of the list that Marybeth and I had made this morning. "It might just be easier to show you this than to try to explain."

She studied the list for a minute, and then Trudy said, "Send this to my phone, would you, please?"

I did as she asked, and twenty seconds later, Trudy was studying the names on her own telephone. After three minutes of frowning at her phone, she looked at me and smiled. "I have some notes for you about your list."

"Go on. I'm listening," I said.

"Okay, first off, it's quite possible that every one of these accusations has a kernel of truth to it," she said. "That might make it a little harder to start paring names off the list."

"Are things really that bad in our little town?" I asked. What had I gotten myself into when I'd moved to be closer to Marybeth? Noble Point certainly hadn't appeared to be a hotbed of crime, but I was beginning to wonder.

"Kelly Madigan steals," Trudy said. "I've been hearing rumors for years about it, but usually her uncle pays off whoever complains about it, so it's not exactly a well-kept secret."

"Who's her uncle?" I asked. I hadn't heard a word about that.

"Actually, you might know him. It's Jim Hicks. He's a local realtor."

"Oh, I know him a little too well," I said.

"That sounds intriguing," Trudy said with a gleam in her eye.

"It's nothing like that. He keeps pressuring me to sell the shop, though."

"You're not considering it, are you?" Trudy asked, clearly appalled by the idea.

"I couldn't even if I wanted to," I said. "Cora left some pretty tight restrictions on what I could do with the place."

"I'm sorry to hear that, but I'm not unhappy that you're staying. You are staying, aren't you?"

"For now," I said. That was all that I was willing to commit to at this point. After I found the murderer, if I ever did, I'd reevaluate my plans, but for now, I wasn't going anywhere.

"Good. You belong in our town. It suits you."

I wasn't going to comment on that, since I wasn't at all sure that I agreed with her. "What about the other names? And is it true what Cora wrote about Jim?"

"If he cheated his former partner, I haven't heard anything about it, with the exception of a few whispers here and there. I need to dig into it a little further before I say one way or the other."

"How about the rest of them?" I asked.

"I don't know the professor, but I should be able to dig something up on him," Trudy said. She pointed to another name. "Celeste's husband refused treatment, over her protests. She tried to sneak him his meds, but he wouldn't hear of it. He wanted to die with whatever dignity he could hold onto, but she wasn't about to give up the fight. It got so bad that Hank started telling anyone who would listen that Celeste was poisoning her food, but in actuality, she was just trying to save his life. Anyone who knew Hank understood, but some folks around here believed him. Cora should have known better, but I suppose it was too juicy to pass up."

I felt relief when I learned that the café owner next door hadn't poisoned her late husband. Celeste and I had gotten off to a bit of a rocky start, but I was finding myself drawn to her the more I got to know her.

You might as well strike a line through the mayor's name as well."

"Did he confess his indiscretions as well?" I asked.

"Oh, no. He was still denying it when his wife caught him in a pretty compromising position with their neighbor. They're heading to divorce court, and I have a hunch that we're going to be getting a new mayor soon," she said with a wicked grin. "Even so, there's no secret to protect there, at least not anymore."

"We're making some real progress," I said. "Anything else?"

"I shouldn't say anything, but I've never been a fan of David Whitman. We dated in high school, and let's just say that it didn't end well. He was a momma's boy then, and he's still one today, as far as I'm concerned. I'll look into his liquidity to see just how desperate he is for money. As for Sandy or Mandy, neither one of them has the gumption to confront anyone directly. I doubt they had the nerve to confront Cora in her shop, no matter what their incentive might be. Now I full well believe that they'd sue anyone for anything, but face to face? I don't believe it." Trudy studied the list again, and then she said, "I seem to have left you with four names. I can surely do better than that."

"You've been a great help so far," I said, and I was about to add something else when the door opened and an older woman with a curler hanging from her hair hurried in.

"I'm so sorry I'm late," she said as she put her oversized handbag on the counter. "I don't know how time got away from me."

"It's fleeting for us all, Elizabeth," Trudy said as she gently removed the offending curler.

"Thanks," Elizabeth said, finally managing to catch her breath a little. "I have a date," she said, the words exploding in the small space.

"That's wonderful," Trudy said in a soft and even voice.

"Who exactly is the lucky fellow?"

Elizabeth's tone matched the librarian's when she replied. "Nathanial Church," she said. "After all these years, he finally got up the nerve to ask me out."

"Good for you," Trudy said. "Would you excuse us, Elizabeth? We have to finish something before Christy opens Memories and Dreams."

"Of course," Elizabeth said as she gathered her handbag up. As she did, one handle came loose from her grip and spilled an enormous amount of flotsam and jetsam onto the counter and the floor below. "I'm such a ditz sometimes," she said as she knelt to start collecting some of her spilled belongings.

As Trudy and I began to help, she said, "I meant that we were going to step outside. Would you watch the desk?"

"I can do that," Elizabeth said. Then she turned to me and added, "I'm usually not so scattered, but there's a great deal riding on this tonight."

"It's fine," I said. "He must be a special fellow."

"He's absolutely dreamy," she said, and then asked me, "Do young people still describe beaus as dreamy?"

"If the shoe fits," I said with a smile.

"I bet you've got someone dreamy yourself," she said.

"Elizabeth," Trudy said sternly. "I'm sure that Christy's love life is none of our concern."

"Or lack thereof," I said with a grin.

"Don't worry, dear," she said as she patted my hand. "Your time will come. I'm sure of it."

Trudy started to laugh at the gesture, but she somehow managed to hold it in until we went outside. "That woman is something else."

"She's just excited about her big date," I said.

"She shouldn't be," Trudy said. "Nathanial Church is as dry as dust. I have no idea why she's so thrilled about dating him."

"To each her own," I said. "Thanks for the help."

"I'm not finished yet," she said. "I'll call you later after

I've done a little digging."

"I don't want to take you from your work," I said.

"It will give me an excuse not to listen to Elizabeth's ramblings," Trudy said with a smile. "I should be the one thanking you for the distraction."

"Call me any time," I said, and then I glanced at my watch. "I've got to get over to the store so I can open it on time. Cora was a real stickler for regular business hours."

"I suppose that's your decision now," Trudy said.

"Maybe, but it will always feel like her shop. I'm a caretaker at best."

"I'm sure things will find a way of working themselves out. They often do."

"I hope you're right," I said.

"I often am," she answered with a smile. "Why should things be different this time? I'll call you soon."

"Thanks so much," I said.

As I started back to the shop, I pulled out my phone and called Marybeth. "Hey, do you have a second for a quick update?"

"You bet. Was she able to help us any?"

"More than I could ask. It turns out that Kelly Madigan shoplifts, but you'll never believe who keeps bailing her out."

"I don't have a clue."

"Jim Hicks. It turns out that he's her uncle."

"Is he the thief Cora claimed?" Marybeth asked.

"She's not sure, so Trudy's going to dig into it a little more, as well as research Professor Jenkins."

Marybeth asked softly, "What about Celeste? Is it possible she killed her husband?"

"No, but I can see how Cora might believe it. Trudy told me that Celeste's husband was dying, and he refused to take his meds. She slipped them into his food, and he caught her. Evidently by the time this happened he was pretty far gone, so he started accusing her of trying to kill him."

"I can see that happening," Marybeth said. "How about

the rest of our list?"

"Trudy doesn't think the sisters would have the guts to confront Cora directly. She's not at all surprised by the lawsuit they're contemplating against me, by the way. Evidently that's the way they work. She thinks that David Whitman might be capable of it if he were desperate enough for money. Trudy's going to dig into that, too."

"Is she even going to have time to do her real job?" Marybeth asked.

"She swears that she's going to be able to fit it in, and I wasn't in any position to say no. We need her help. She's got the connections that we don't."

"Then bless her for doing it. Oh, we can strike the mayor's name off our list. I made a few phone calls myself, and it turns out that he just got caught with his neighbor the night before Cora was murdered, so there wouldn't be any secret for him to protect at that point. That's some real progress, isn't it?"

"You bet it is. As things stand now, we've still got Jim Hicks, David Whitman, Barbara Hastings, and Kelly Madigan on our list of suspects."

"I'm not sure why Kelly is on there. She might be a petty thief, but I doubt that makes her a killer."

"I'm not ready to rule her out yet," I said. "What if Cora caught her stealing and threatened to turn her over to the police? Kelly might have done it to keep from going to jail."

"Maybe. Listen, try not to do anything crazy until I get back, okay? We can't forget that we're dealing with a murderer here."

"It's not about to slip my mind," I said, thinking of not just Cora, but Midnight as well.

"Sorry, I didn't mean anything by that."

"No worries," I said. "Let me know when you get back into town."

"I will," she said, and we hung up.

I'd been hoping for a little quiet time before I had to

open, but when I saw who was waiting for me outside Memories and Dreams, I knew that wasn't going to happen.

It appeared that one of my suspects had decided to visit me today before I even had the chance to unlock the front door.

"Hello, Jim," I said as I fumbled for my keys. "I'm sorry, but I'm not open for business quite yet."

"I'm not here to shop," he said. "I've been speaking with a first-class attorney, and he assures me that we can circumvent whatever clauses Cora inserted into the will. You're free and clear to sell the place."

"Unlike you, *I'm* not interested in going against Cora's last wishes. I'm not selling, and that's final."

Jim clearly didn't like that. "You know, it's not that easy running a business like this. Bad things can happen." The last bit was said with a chilling tone that I didn't care for at all.

"Is that a threat, Jim?" I asked.

He frowned, and then shook his head. "I don't threaten. I just think you should be aware of the downside of hanging onto this place."

"Funny, that sounds an awful lot like a threat to me. Is that how you got away with stealing so much money from your former business partner?"

His gaze narrowed. "I don't know what you're talking about."

"Oh, I sincerely doubt that. How much did you clear after all of the dust settled in the end?" I was pushing him hard, and I knew it, but I needed to get things rolling. I knew that the longer it took to solve the murders, the harder it was going to be.

Jim took a step closer to me, and for one crazy second I thought he was going to hit me. Instead, in a voice that was barely containing his rage, he said, "You need to drop it, and I mean now."

"What if I don't?" I asked, hoping that someone was nearby if I needed some help.

"This is your last chance," he said.

The words reminded me of the note I'd found that someone had written to Cora. "Is that what you told my friend just before she was murdered? Were you trying to force her into selling, too? Is that what happened when she refused you?"

I knew I'd pushed too far with my last statement. Instead of protesting or trying to deny anything, Jim turned and walked away without another word. If he was the killer, I'd just given him enough incentive to get rid of me. Nice going, Christy.

My hands were shaking as I fit the key into the lock, and I wondered if my last mistake of pushing the man too hard would end up being a fatal one.

Chapter 13

Things were quiet at the shop for the next hour, and I was beginning to wonder if there was any reason to stay open when the front door opened. When Kelly Madigan walked in, my spirits fell a little. After the confrontation I'd just had with her uncle, I wasn't in the mood to deal with her at the moment.

She approached me, her gaze downward. "Christy, I came by to apologize for being so snippy with you before."

That was a surprise. "I appreciate that," I said.

"Good. Now, if you don't mind, I think I'll look around a little."

"That's fine. After all, that's why we're here."

It wasn't that funny, but Kelly managed to laugh too long and too loudly, and it made me wonder if there was something else on her mind. I started rearranging some of the jewelry in the display case when I happened to glance up just in time to see Kelly tucking a black beret into her purse. It was marked for sale at a dollar, and she was stealing from me! I fought the urge to confront her on the spot and pretended not to notice what she'd done. After a few minutes, Kelly approached me and smiled. "Nothing struck my fancy today, but who knows? I'll be back tomorrow. See you."

She was nearly out the door when I reached out and grabbed her shoulder. "Aren't you forgetting something?"

"What are you talking about? I already apologized," she said defensively.

"Yes, and I accepted it. What I refuse to accept, though, is someone stealing from me. I saw you take that beret, Kelly."

If she'd been the one who had attacked Cora and Midnight, I was pretty confident that I'd see something now.

I braced myself for an attack, so I was quite surprised

when she started crying. They weren't soft and simpering tears either, but a deluge that nearly doubled her over.

"Get control of yourself," I snapped. Was I going to have to slap her to get her to stop crying?

"I'm so sorry," she said. "I have a sickness. Call my uncle, he'll tell you."

The last thing I wanted was to invite Jim Hicks into my shop. "I think I'll call the police instead," I said.

That pushed her the rest of the way over the edge. Kelly collapsed on the floor, and I raced around to see if I could help her. Based on her reaction to our confrontation, I couldn't imagine that she'd attack Cora or Midnight under any circumstances. The real question now was what was I going to do with her?

"Get up, Kelly," I ordered. I gave it every ounce of command I could summon in my voice, and something in my tone hit home.

She stood, retrieved the beret, and then put it on the counter, along with a twenty-dollar bill. "Can I go now?" she asked as though she were a child asking permission to leave the table.

"Not quite," I said, refusing to touch the beret or the money. "You can't keep stealing, you know that, don't you?"

"I try to fight it, but sometimes it's too hard, especially when I'm so stressed out."

"You're going to have to figure out a better way to cope with it than shoplifting," I said.

"Please don't call the police. I'm begging you!"

I had my hand on the phone, but could I do it? She sounded so pathetic, but then again, she'd tried to steal from me, and as the shopkeeper, I couldn't allow that. Then again, if I had her arrested for a beret that cost a dollar, what might that do to my business? Morally, I wanted to call the sheriff, but pragmatically, I didn't really need the hassle of having her arrested in my shop over such a trivial amount. I finally came to a decision, and took the beret, but left the twenty.

"Go on. Take your money."

She looked at me, trying to see if I was messing with her, but when she saw my expression, she took the money and raced for the door.

Before she could get there, though, I said, "You are not allowed to come back here, and I mean ever. If you step across that threshold again, I'll call the police and have you arrested. Do you understand me?"

Kelly looked shocked by the banishment. "You can't do that!"

"You bet I can," I said.

"You don't even have any proof that I took anything," Kelly said, her voice a bit cloying as she spoke.

"You must not have seen my new security camera," I said as I pointed to the ceiling. She looked up, and I could see her shake her head in disbelief. I smiled at her, but there was no warmth in it. "Oh, yes." Had I remembered to even turn it on this morning? I wasn't sure, but then again, as far as Kelly was concerned, her theft had been captured there.

She left the shop without another word. I was having second thoughts about just letting her go like that, but maybe my punishment had been more severe than what the police would have done over a dollar item. In my view, stealing was stealing, but this was the best compromise I'd been able to come up with. One thing was fairly certain. Kelly wasn't a killer, at least not according to what I'd seen earlier. I felt confident taking her off our list. I had a hunch she'd been upset about the necklace I was now wearing because she'd lost her opportunity to steal it for herself. If she wouldn't pay a single dollar for a cheap beret, she wasn't about to fork over a few hundred for a necklace.

Thinking of the necklace made me suddenly realize that there might be a way to eliminate or highlight another one of our suspects. I decided to phone David Whitman and see just how desperate he was to get it back.

"Mr. Whitman, this is Christy from Memories and Dreams."

"Who? Oh, the girl I spoke to before. What can I do for you?"

"I'm calling about the necklace your mother sold us," I said. "I've been able to track it down, and the buyer is willing to sell it back to you for what she paid for it." Of course I was lying through my teeth, but David Whitman had no way of knowing that. If he was agreeable, I'd broker a deal without taking a profit, and then I'd see if I could pick something a lot less volatile, with Lincoln's permission.

"Thank you, but after speaking with my mother, we've decided not to pursue it," he said.

I hadn't been sure what kind of reaction I'd get from my offer, but I certainly hadn't been expecting that. "Are you sure?" I asked.

"I'm positive," he said. "Now, if there's nothing else, I'm late for a meeting."

"That's it," I said.

After we hung up, I tried to figure out why he'd changed his mind so abruptly. And then one scenario came unwillingly to mind. What if David Whitman was going to report that the necklace in question had been stolen, and not sold? It was outright fraud, there was no doubt about that, but I couldn't prove anything unless the insurance adjuster came to me and asked about the necklace, and that wasn't going to happen. They wouldn't even know that Cora had bought it. What was wrong with these people? I suddenly didn't want to have anything to do with the necklace anymore, even if Lincoln wouldn't allow me to change my mind. It had bad karma as far as I was concerned, and I didn't want to wear it a minute longer. I took it off, and as I did, the phone rang.

"Hello?" I asked as I put it in the display case.

"It's David Whitman. I've changed my mind. How much are you asking for it?"

What was going on here? I decided to push things a little to see what he'd say. "You're going to have to double the original hundred we paid for it," I said.

"That's quite a markup," Whitman said. "Do you have any wiggle room on that price?"

"What did you have in mind?" I asked.

"I'll give you a hundred and fifty, but I don't want a receipt. In fact, I insist on it."

"I'm sorry, but we are required by law to keep track of the used jewelry we sell. The records go to the police at the end of every month so they can check their records against insurance claims that are made." This too was a lie, but I was dying to see what David Whitman thought of this new development.

After a long hesitation, he said, "But this isn't being sold; it's being returned to its original owner. How about if we double it and make it three hundred if you forget to file the paperwork? Does that interest you?"

"Not one little bit," I said. "Besides, we never agreed on one-fifty. My price was and is two hundred dollars, and I'm giving you a huge break as it is."

"Are you actually going to try to hold me up for more?" he asked.

"No, that's not it at all. I just don't want to take a loss on this." What was next? I wondered.

"Okay," he said with some resignation in his voice. "You drive a hard bargain. Two hundred, and you file all of the reports you want to. I'll be down this afternoon to pick it up. I trust it will be there."

"It sure will, but you need to bring cash with you," I said, remembering what I had heard about his money problems.

"That's an odd request, isn't it?" he asked. "Do you make all of your customers pay you in cash?"

"Call me quirky, but it's the only way you're getting the necklace back. I've got to pay my buyer today, and I won't make her wait for the money until your check clears."

"Fine," he said, and then he hung up on me before I could say anything else.

While the shop would make a tidy profit on the sale, it could have been a great deal more, but I drew the line at extorting too much cash from our customers, no matter how sleazy they seemed to be to me.

I was losing faith in David Whitman as a suspect. He might have money problems, but I doubted the necklace would come anywhere close to solving them, not if what Cora had written about him was true. While I couldn't take his name off the list entirely, it did make me wonder if I was following a bad lead by pursuing him as one of my suspects.

When the front door opened next, I expected to see David Whitman come in. Instead, it was Jim Hicks, and there were too many ways that I wasn't happy about his presence in my shop than I could count.

I was about to snap when I noticed his smile. It was the first real one I'd seen since I'd met the man. What did he have to be so happy about all of a sudden? "What can I do for you?" I asked him.

"Actually, I came to thank you. I just spoke to Kelly. Thank you for not calling the police. I can't tell you how much I appreciate it."

"I'll be honest with you; I'm having second thoughts. She stole from me, plain and simple. How have you managed to keep her out of jail this long?"

"Many of the shop owners have been very understanding in the past," he said. "She's getting much better, if it's any consolation."

"Well, it's nice. I suppose you'd like me to lift my ban of her from this store."

I was about to give him all of the reasons that I wouldn't change my mind when he surprised me. "That was a stroke of brilliance. I don't know what you said to her, but she's terrified that she'll never be able to come back. It might just prove to be enough to allow her to stop once and forever. She used to be a fine, upstanding young girl, and then her parents died in a horrible car accident. She came to live with me when she was nine, and the poor kid has been scarred for life by the trauma of losing them both so suddenly."

"Have you tried to get her help?" I asked. I hadn't realized what she'd been through, but at least in my mind, that still didn't excuse her thefts.

"We're still looking for the right answer for her," he said. "But I believe that we are finally getting close. She's been good for months. I don't know what triggered her today, but she assures me that it won't happen again."

"Well, I can guarantee that it won't, at least not here. I can't afford to have my merchandise keep disappearing."

"About that," Jim said as he pulled a hundred dollar bill out of his wallet. "This should more than make up for the trouble."

"I wouldn't take Kelly's twenty, and I'm not going to accept your hundred, either. What's she going to learn if you keep buying her out of trouble?" I was lecturing the man, and I hated the sound of my voice as I did, but somebody had to say these things to him, no matter how hard it was for all of the parties involved.

"Fair enough," he said as he tucked the bill back into his wallet. "May I at least buy the beret in question?"

"I'm not exactly sure that's the right signal, either, are you?"

"I want it as a reminder to her that she can't just steal things when she's feeling frustrated or alone. It's a valuable lesson, don't you think?"

"I do. In fact," I said, "let the beret be my gift to you both. A dollar profit is worth losing if it helps her straighten herself out."

"I can't accept this," he said as I put the hat in a bag and handed it to him.

"Don't make me call the police," I said, adding a grin so he could see that I was just teasing.

"We don't want that," he said as he took it from me. "Thank you for your understanding, and your compassion."

"It's just a dollar," I said, uneasy with his praise.

"It means a great deal more than that to us," he said. "I won't be bothering you any more about selling this place.

You've at least earned that from me today."

"Then I'm the one who's coming out ahead," I said.

"What's that?" Jim asked as he looked at the counter. I'd shoved Cora's notebook under a bag, and when I'd given the hat to him, the journal was suddenly exposed.

I put it under the counter as I said, "It's just some of my musings."

"I didn't know that you were a writer," Jim said with a smile.

"I'm not. At least not yet. Someday, maybe."

"I'm certain of it," he said. Holding the bagged hat aloft, he said, "Thank you again for your kindness."

"She deserved one warning, but that's all that she's going to get from me," I said.

"I'm sure that will be sufficient," he said, and then the real estate agent pulled out a sales flyer and folded it in half. After jotting something down, he handed it to me. "This is my cell number. I owe you one, so if there's anything I can do for you, call me."

"Thanks, but I can't imagine the circumstances."

"Still, you've got it if you need it," he said, and then Jim Hicks left the shop. I put the flyer on the counter and promptly forgot all about it.

Lincoln came in ten seconds later. "I'm here to take you to lunch," he said. "Hey, was that who I thought it was leaving your shop just now? Jim Hicks isn't still pestering you about selling this place to him, is he?"

"No. As a matter of fact, he told me that he's asked for the last time."

"And do you believe him?" Lincoln asked.

"Where there's life, there's hope." That's when the other shoe dropped about Lincoln's appearance. "You're here for lunch."

"Is that a question, or a statement?" he asked.

"I can't. I'm so sorry, but there's no way I can leave the shop. Is that okay?"

"It's fine," he said, and then Lincoln headed for the door.

"That doesn't mean that you have to just rush off," I said. Had I hurt his feelings with my rejection?

Lincoln just smiled as he walked away. I'd blown it now. Just when things were starting to look promising, I'd run him off. I was sad to admit to myself that it wasn't the first time, and I was fairly sure that it wouldn't be the last, either. Oh, well. Such was the life of a single shopkeeper.

I had to eat something, though. I started to make a sign that I could put in the window that said I'd be gone for ten minutes when Lincoln surprised me by coming back in, this time holding a large brown bag in his hands. "If you can't go to lunch, then lunch will come to you," he said with a smile.

"You didn't have to do that," I said with a smile. What was I smelling, Celeste's French fries? I could feel myself drooling at the very thought of them.

"I didn't have to," Lincoln said. "I wanted to. Where shall we dine?"

"How about back here behind the counter?" I asked. "Is that okay with you?"

"I'll go wherever you'd like me to," he said. "Now, what say we start our little feast before we're interrupted?"

"I think that's a marvelous plan. What are we having?" I asked as I peeked into the bag.

"Two hamburgers, two fries, and two sodas," he said as he started withdrawing food from the bag. "Do those selections meet with your approval?"

"More than you could ever know. I'm starving," I said as I reached greedily for one of the burgers.

"I managed to work up quite an appetite myself," Lincoln said.

"How was court this morning?" I asked, and then I took a bite my mother would have never approved of. Well, she wasn't around to critique my eating habits, so I was going to eat as it pleased me.

"My client was a complete and total boob," Lincoln said. "He got caught robbing a convenience store, and then, to make matters worse, he tried to steal the police cruiser they placed him in upon his arrest."

"How did he manage that?" I asked, trying not to laugh.

"One of the officers failed to secure his door properly, so while their backs were turned, he calmly got out, walked around to the driver's door, and got in."

"How far did he get?" I asked, this time failing to conceal my laughter.

"Not a foot. It turns out that he doesn't know how to drive."

"Why didn't he just run away, if they weren't paying any attention to him?" I asked.

"The very question I asked him myself. He claimed that they were trying to entrap him, so he wanted to show the world just how devious the police are."

"What happened to him?"

"He'll be out on bail in a few days, but after that, he's on his own. I was filling in for a colleague, so after this, they're both on their own."

"You're a lifesaver," I said as I took another healthy bite of my burger. "It's good to have a guy like you around."

Lincoln's back stiffened, and I wondered what I'd said. "Hey, that was a compliment, in case you didn't know."

"Christy, you sounded as though the next words that were going to come out of your mouth was what a good friend I am."

I'd been close. "What would be so bad about that?"

"Pardon me for saying so, but I have enough friends, thank you very much. I like you, and not in a way that could be misconstrued as friendship. Let me say it simply, and boldly. I have a romantic interest in dating you, and if things go well, I may even try to woo you. Would you be opposed to that?"

"I don't know, I haven't been wooed in a long time," I said.

"Are you making fun of me?" he asked with carefully chosen words.

"No, I think it's kind of sweet, to be honest with you. Okay, go ahead. Woo me. Let's see where it goes."

"First we try a date or two, and then I'll decide if there's any wooing in our future." He said it with a grin, and I responded in kind.

"We'll try a few dates, then, but you be sure to tell me if we advance to the wooing stage."

"Oh, believe me, you'll know." He stood, and then cleaned up the bags. "Where should I put these?"

"There's a trash can in back," I said. "But just leave it. I can take care of it later."

"I respectfully decline your offer," he said. Sometimes talking to him was like a trip back in time, but in all honestly, I kind of liked it.

He was gone ten seconds when my phone rang. I was about to let it go to voice mail when I saw that it was Trudy from the library.

"Hey, Trudy. Give me one second, would you?"

"I can give you three, if you need them," she said with a laugh.

I walked into the back as Lincoln was walking back in, and we nearly collided in the doorway. For one second, he had his arms around me to keep me from falling, and I had to admit that I didn't mind it, not one bit. "I'm so sorry, but I have a call I need to take."

"I understand," he said. "Are you busy tonight?"

"I'm not sure yet. May I call you?"

"I'll wait, but not forever," he said with a grin.

After he was gone, I could still smell traces of his cologne in the air. Snapping myself out of it, I put my phone back to my ear and said, "Sorry about that. Someone was here."

"Someone tall, dark, and handsome, I hope?" she asked.

"I suppose you could say that. How's the search been going?"

Trudy laughed. "So, that's all of the details I'm getting out of you. Is that right?"

"Pretty much," I agreed.

"I understand," she said. "I just called to tell you that Professor Jenkins has an unshakable alibi, so he needs to be taken off your list."

"I'd love to hear what it is," I said.

"On that fateful day, he was at a conference on the west coast. I called a few places to confirm it, and it's true."

"Trudy, did you come right out and ask him for his alibi?" The woman had more moxie than I did, that was for sure.

"Of course not. I spoke to a secretary at the college, and she told me. We took a class together in continuing education once."

"Dare I ask what the subject was?"

"We were both getting our scuba diving certifications, as a matter of fact," Trudy said. "Wendy was going on vacation to the Bahamas."

"How about you?"

"It just sounded like fun to me," she said. The woman had levels that I was just discovering, and the deeper I dug, the more I liked her.

"Do you trust her?"

"I do, but that's not an issue. I went online and downloaded his lecture. It was time and date stamped, so there's no discussion. He's in the clear."

"Thank you so much," I said. "You should get a merit badge in detection."

"I'm a librarian. What makes you think that I don't already have one?" she asked me. "I've got to run. I have a few more feelers out, so sit tight. We'll have this thing solved in no time."

"I have a hunch that the police don't know what a valuable asset they are missing out on," I said.

"Oh, they know," she said, and I could hear the grin in her voice as she said it.

Chapter 14

I suddenly realized that I'd forgotten to ask Lincoln if I could choose something else for my legacy. Taking a chance, I called his cell phone.

"Do you miss me already?" he asked after he picked up. "I'm taking that as a good sign, whether you mean it to be or not."

"I have a question for you," I said.

"Ask away. As it happens, I'm still free tonight, if that's why you're calling."

"It's not, but I can appreciate a man who looks at things from a positive point of view. Can I change my mind about my inheritances from Cora?"

"Have you decided to swap the wooden box for something more valuable?"

"As a matter of fact, I want to keep the box," I said. "It's the necklace I was thinking about trading in."

"Sure, that would be fine, but may I ask why?"

"I'm selling it back to David Whitman," I said.

"You're not under any obligation to do that. You realize that, don't you? Has he been bullying you about it?"

"I brought it up myself. With all of the ill will surrounding it, I don't feel right taking it for myself."

"Understood. I at least hope you're gouging him for more than the hundred Cora bought it for."

"I doubled my money," I said with a smile.

Lincoln laughed. "It looks as though there might be a bit of Cora in you after all." After a moment's pause, he quickly added, "Sorry. I shouldn't have said that last bit."

"Don't apologize. It's one of the nicest things you've ever said to me," I said.

"Have you made a new selection?" Lincoln asked me.

"I'm still thinking about it," I said.

"Well, just let me know so I can change the paperwork.

If you'd like help deciding, I'd be happy to lend my expertise in fine antiques and jewelry tonight."

"You're trying to skip dating and go straight to wooing, are you?" I asked with a laugh.

"No, Ma'am. The formalities must be followed. I'll talk to you later."

"Bye," I said.

When I hung up, I saw Midnight for a split second. It must have been harder for him to appear in broad daylight, but he was still there long enough for me to see him shaking his head at me, something he'd often done when he'd been in firmer form.

Wonderful. Only one of my cats would find a way to make fun of me from beyond the Great Divide.

In the middle of the afternoon, my cell phone rang. It was Marybeth. "Have you heard from our friend the librarian yet?"

"Actually, she called while I was having lunch with Lincoln."

"Hang on a second. You had lunch with Lincoln?" she asked. "I want to hear every last detail."

"Marybeth, why don't we talk about that later? Let's focus on the case right now. Trudy said that Professor Jenkins is off our list of suspects, no matter how much interest he showed in that wooden box."

"How could he have an alibi that tight?" Marybeth asked.

"He was speaking at a conference on the west coast when everything happened here," I said.

"Do you have any proof besides his word that he actually went?"

"There's a posted video of his presentation on the internet, and it is date and time stamped," I said.

"Okay then, we'll mark him off our list. Did anything else happen?"

"Actually, it's been a pretty eventful day. When I got here to open the shop, Jim Hicks was waiting for me, and unless I'm grossly mistaken, he threatened me."

"Now we're talking," Marybeth said. "What kind of threat was it?"

"On a scale of one to ten, I'd say that it was about a six."

"That doesn't sound like all that much of a threat to me."

"That's just part of it. Kelly Madigan came in, and I caught her trying to steal a beret. When I called her on it, she broke down."

"Did you call the police?" Marybeth asked.

"I thought about it, but given that I've just taken the shop over, I wasn't sure that was the kind of publicity I wanted. I did ban her from the store for life, though."

"That might be a better punishment after all," she said.

"Jim Hicks came in later, and the man actually apologized! He promised that he'd drop his pursuit of my shop, and that we were good."

"Did you believe him?" Marybeth asked.

"I did. He loves his niece, and after hearing her story, I understand things a little better."

"Are you ready to take them off our list, then?"

I thought about it, and then I replied, "After confronting Kelly, I don't think she'd be capable of murder. Jim made some progress with me, but I'm not ready to cross his name off our list just yet."

"So, where does that leave us?"

"As far as I'm concerned, Jim is still there, along with Barbara Hastings, and to a lesser degree, David Whitman, though I'll know his status better when he comes here later to buy my necklace."

"Hang on," Marybeth said. "You're going to sell one of the things you got from Cora?"

"She never actually gave it to me," I said. "Given the circumstances, I don't want to keep it. Lincoln told me that I could pick something else out, though."

"Let me help you this time," she said.

"Don't you trust my taste?"

"You picked out a wooden box, remember?"

I wasn't about to tell her that had been my ghost cat's idea. "It had sentimental value."

"Well, let's pick something out that has some actual worth. Only it can't be tonight. That's the real reason I'm calling. I have to go to Asheville for an emergency meeting with my boss. Her boss is putting some pressure on her to find out why sales are down, and I've been summoned to the meeting to testify. I don't know why they want to talk to me. My numbers have never looked better. Anyway, I may end up staying there overnight."

"At least you have your travel bag," I said. Marybeth always kept a backup outfit in her car in case of emergencies, and this clearly qualified in her world.

"I'm all set. I'll probably see you tomorrow. Christy, don't do anything I wouldn't do, okay?"

"Is there anything that actually makes that list?" I asked with a laugh.

"There are a few things, but I doubt you'll get that far down the list. See you later."

"Good luck," I said.

"Thanks, but I think my boss is going to be the one who needs it."

"I've got to go," I said as David Whitman came into the shop.

"Call me later," she said, but I didn't answer.

"Do you have the necklace?" he asked.

"That depends. Do you have the money?"

He fanned a handful of twenties out on the counter. I half suspected he'd try to cheat me, but it totaled up to two hundred dollars. I grabbed the necklace and handed it over to him. After a quick examination, he stuffed it into his pocket.

"Do you need a bag for that?"

"There's no reason to bother with that."

"Hang on," I said as he started to leave. "I'm required by law to write you a receipt."

"Throw it away when you're done with it, then," he said gruffly. "I told you before. I don't want one."

"You're not planning on doing anything illegal, are you?" I asked him.

That managed to freeze him in his tracks. "What are you talking about?"

"I understand the police frown on insurance fraud," I said. "I'd hate to see anything happen to you just because you were out of money."

"Who told you that?" he asked sharply.

"The word's out," I said. "The entire town knows."

Whitman frowned, and then he looked as though he wanted to spit on my clean floor. "They don't know half as much as they think they do," he said. "Sure, I ran into a temporary cash flow problem last month, but it's all worked itself out."

"So, you're saying that you're not broke?"

"That's exactly what I'm saying," he replied. "What is it with you people? First Cora accuses me of being shady, and now you're questioning my finances. I'll tell you what I told her. It's nobody's business but mine. And while we're talking, there's one more thing that I need to say. You are not allowed to buy anything else from my mother, no matter what she says. If you do, I'll make sure that it's the last thing you buy. Do you read me?"

"Loud and clear," I said. "My, you've got quite the temper, don't you?"

"You don't know the half of it," he said, and then David Whitman stormed out of the shop. Had I hit a nerve? I didn't believe him for a second. The man was clearly up to something. I just wasn't sure that it had anything to do with Cora and Midnight.

One thing I was sure of. The man was still on my list. In fact, he may have just vaulted to the number-one position.

There was one suspect on our list that I hadn't had a chance to speak with yet. Barbara Hastings' name had come up in Cora's notebook, and the scandal attached to her name might be enough to cause her to kill to protect her secret. I couldn't make her come to the shop, but I could do the next best thing. It went against everything that Cora believed, but I felt as though she would have made an exception if she could have. I was going to close the shop in the midst of a workday and go looking for my final suspect.

I scrawled a quick note, stuck it in the window by the door, locked the place up, and went off in search of Barbara Hastings.

I found her at home; at least that was something. Barbara lived in a two-story colonial with a tumbled brick exterior.

When she came to the door, she looked worn and a little frazzled. "You're not Cindy," she said when she saw me.

"No, my name's Christy. I've taken over Memories and Dreams. Do you have a second to chat?"

"Not really. If I don't leave in the next minute, I'll be late picking up my children from school, and I can't afford to let that happen."

"Is it because of what happened with the PTA?" I asked, hoping that Cora had been right about that.

She crumpled instantly, and I regretted the way I'd just sprung it on her. "It's never going to end, is it? I paid them back every dime I took, I made a full confession to the board in exchange for them agreeing not to prosecute me, and they promised not to press charges or tell anyone about it. How did you find out?"

"It's a small town," I said apologetically. I hated the thought of ambushing her like that, even if what she'd done had been so utterly wrong. She'd stolen from the children of our community, and paying the money back didn't sound like a fair restitution to me.

"I should have known that I wouldn't be able to stay here," Barbara said as she wiped her tears away. "It's been two of the longest weeks of my life, and if anything, it's just gotten worse since then."

"Are you telling me that this all happened two weeks ago?" I asked.

"It feels like a lifetime, but yes, it was two weeks ago to

the day that everything started to collapse. Now if you'll excuse me, I've got to pick up my kids and then start making plans to leave town."

"You could always stay and just ride it out. It won't be easy, but you can do it," I said.

"That's the pipedream I had before my world came crashing down. My husband left me yesterday, did you know that?"

"I didn't," I admitted.

"He couldn't stand the thought of being married to a common thief. It doesn't mean a thing that he cheats people every day for his job. No, *I'm* the pariah." She stepped out and locked the door behind her. "Excuse me, but why exactly are you here?"

"I'm going door to door telling folks about the changes I'm making at my shop," I said. It was the first thing that came to mind, and it was so tissue-thin that under other circumstances, it wouldn't have stood a chance.

"Well, in case you haven't gotten the complete picture, I'm broke and alone. I couldn't even afford the things you carry. That's how far I've fallen."

I watched as she drove away, and then headed back to the shop. If what Barbara had just told me was true, and I had no reason to doubt her, then she had been exposed and punished long before Cora and Midnight had been attacked.

At that point, there had been no reason for her to come after them.

That took one more name off my list, and I was beginning to wonder if the sheriff might know something that we didn't. Was the real killer one of the two people left on our list, or was it someone else entirely? I didn't have access to what the sheriff was thinking, but I had no real choice in the matter.

I had to keep digging, and until I could clear both Jim Hicks and David Whitman, I still had to believe that I had a viable suspect list.

The question was how to determine which one of them

might be the murderer.

As I was closing up for the night, I glanced at the counter and saw Midnight again in all of his glory. He was pouncing up and down, a sure sign that he was agitated. "What's wrong, Big Guy?" I asked.

Instead of answering me, he started scratching at the counter with his ghostly nails. It was kind of eerie watching his vigorous movements that resulted in nothing at all. "Are you trying to tell me something?"

"Merwerer," he said emphatically.

I walked toward him, and I expected him to vanish, but he stayed exactly where he was.

"I'm sorry, but I can't bring myself to reach through you," I said.

He shook his head once, and then stepped aside. He might not have approved of my squeamishness, but at least he'd understood.

I picked up the paper on top of the pile and saw that it was the sales flyer that Jim Hicks had left me. "Is this what you wanted me to look at?" I asked.

"Mewr," he said, nodding once.

A sudden chill swept through me. "Is he the one who hurt you?" I asked. The question nearly stuck in my throat as I asked it.

"Merw," he said solemnly, a yes if I'd ever heard one.

"I'm so sorry," I said, and forgetting myself for a second, I tried to comfort him by stroking his back.

I could swear that for one second, my hand made real contact before Midnight disappeared.

Okay, I believed my cat, though I couldn't tell that to anyone else. He'd just named his murderer.

What was I going to do about it, though?

I was still trying to come up with a plan when my phone rang.

I nearly jumped out of my skin when it did.

Marybeth asked, "Are you okay?"

"I'm fine," I said. "Why do you ask?"

"I just got the weirdest feeling about you. My uncle just called. It appears that our investigation is over."

"What happened?"

"They are arresting David Whitman in a few minutes for fraud and attempted murder. He tried to shove his mother down the stairs to make it look like an accident. Can you believe that?"

Remembering the man's temper, I had no trouble buying that he could have done just that. "That's pretty horrific, but what does it have to do with us?"

"My uncle told me that they're pretty sure that he killed Cora and Midnight, too. He was seen near the shop half an hour before it happened, and he had more than that necklace on him when they arrested him."

"Something else from my shop?" I asked.

"That's why the police will be calling on you soon. They need you to identify a pair of diamond earrings they believe were stolen during the robbery."

"We haven't had any diamond earrings for months," I said.

"Well, regardless of that, he believes that he has the right man."

I didn't, but I couldn't tell Marybeth that my dearly departed cat had named someone else as he killer. "Great."

"You don't sound all that convinced," she said.

"It's just a shock hearing what he just did," I said.

"Are you sure you're okay?"

"I'm fine," I said. I didn't believe that David Whitman had killed Cora and Midnight for a second, but I also didn't want to spend another moment arguing with Marybeth about it.

"Well, I thought you'd be pleased. I'll see you tomorrow."

"Thanks for calling," I said.

After we hung up, Nancy Glade walked in, carrying something in her hands as though it was priceless. "This is your lucky day, Christy. I've got something really nice for you today." Nancy loved to haunt flea markets in the area, and she had constantly brought in items she thought were of value, only to have Cora tell her that her items were nearly worthless.

I did my best to smile. "Let's see it."

"You like cats, don't you?" Nancy asked before she would hand it over.

"You know I do," I said.

"Then you're going to love this," she said as she handed me a hard glass snow globe. There was a black cat in its center, and I felt a tug thinking about Midnight. "Go on. Shake it up."

I did as she asked and saw the cat suddenly surrounded by swirling patterns of white. No self-respecting cat I ever knew would allow themselves to be caught out in a snowstorm, but I didn't have the heart to tell her that. "It's cute," I said.

"It's more than that," Nancy said. "It's art."

I wasn't about to debate that with her for a second. "How much are you asking?"

"I think it's worth ten dollars at least," she said.

I raised an eyebrow and flipped it over. Someone had put a piece of tape on the bottom, and they'd marked the price at one dollar. "That's quite a markup you're asking for there."

"Oops." She quickly peeled off the tape as though it would erase the price I'd just seen from my memory as well. "How about five?"

"I'll give you two," I said. "That way you can double your money."

"Oh, it's worth more than that," she said cagily.

"Well, I hope you have luck getting it."

I tried to hand the snow globe back to her, but she wouldn't take it. "Hey, we're still dickering here, aren't we? How about two-fifty?"

"Sold," I said. It was worth that just to end the haggling. I gave her the money, wrote her a receipt, and then said,

"We're closing early tonight. Thanks for stopping in."

"I'll be back tomorrow," she said, and I didn't doubt it for a second. After she left, I realized that I wasn't making any progress at the shop. Maybe it was time to do what I'd promised Nancy and go back home. If nothing else, it would be a real pleasure to see Shadow again. He'd been keeping himself scarce lately, but I believed that we both needed time together right now more than ever. I put the snow globe down after giving it another shake. Nancy was right; the glass was heavy, not the cheap plastic many snow globes were made of these days. I decided to mark it for sale at five dollars and see if I got any takers. I'd find a place for it tomorrow, but for now, it would work just fine as a paperweight.

"Shadow, I'm home," I said as I walked into the house.

No greeting from either cat, which was not that big of a surprise. I got some of his food out and put it on the floor in the kitchen, and then I proceeded to heat up some soup. I wasn't in the mood to cook, so it was good enough to eat. Halfway through my meal, I heard a noise at my feet, hoping it was Midnight.

It wasn't. Shadow had joined me after all. I finished eating, and then waited for him. Meal time was one instance I *never* interfered with my cats. After he finished, he looked up at me, licked his lips once, and then asked, "Mew?"

"Sure, hop on up," I said as I made room for him on my lap. Shadow leapt up in an elegant fashion, and then he bumped my chin once before settling down. As I stroked his coat, I said, "I'm sorry I haven't been very good company lately. You've had it worse than me."

"Mwerr," he said, and I supplied my own interpretation of his comment.

"Okay, we are suffering equally, but I should have been better with you. I resolve to change from this moment forward."

His reply was a quick sneeze, and then without warning,

Shadow jumped to the floor. "Hey, where are you going?" I asked, but I didn't get a reply. I loved that about my cats. They made a fuss when they saw me, but when it was time to go off on other explorations, they never thought twice about saying good-bye. I would have loved to be more like them, but I'd never mastered their art of aloof behavior.

"How about you, Midnight? Are you here?" I asked.

There was a sound from the front parlor, and I hurried out there in anticipation.

Nobody was there, not a live cat or a ghost one either.

It may have been Midnight, but most likely, it was just my imagination. I sat on the sofa and turned on the television, flipping through the channels at an alarming rate before I ended up turning it off again. After I put the remote control down, I picked up a book I'd been reading, but after repeating the same sentence three times, I set that aside, too. I was restless, and there wasn't anything I could really do about it.

As I sat there in silence, I started wondering how I could trap Jim Hicks into confessing his crimes. The man would be a tough nut to crack, but there had to be a way to do it. Should I use my threat against Kelly Madigan to force him into telling the truth, or I'd have her arrested? Even if it might work, I couldn't bring myself to try it. I didn't approve of Kelly's behavior by any stretch of the imagination, but her circumstances were somewhat extenuating. I was glad I wasn't a judge, because I had no idea how to balance that particular scale of justice. When it came to the person who had taken away my best friend and my boss, I wasn't about to be so forgiving, though. I wanted justice for Midnight and Cora, not revenge. There had to be a way of bringing Jim Hicks down without involving Kelly Madigan. The only real resource I had besides Trudy was the journal Cora had kept. Could I have missed something she'd written there? Why hadn't I brought it home with me tonight? I sat there another ten minutes stewing about it, and then I decided that I wasn't going to get any rest tonight unless I had that book, so I grabbed a jacket and headed back out. At least I hadn't had to explain my behavior to Marybeth. She was gone for the night, and I was on my own. As I drove to the shop, I thought about the last time I'd come there late at night on foot. I'd been with Midnight, following him down the darkened streets, and I wished I had him beside me. Unfortunately, that wasn't in my power.

I unlocked the door, slipped inside without relocking it, and entered the combination to disarm the alarm system Emily had installed for me.

It started beeping that all was safe, and as I reached for the door, it was jerked out of my hands.

Jim Hicks stood there scowling at me, and worse yet, he had a gun pointed straight at my heart.

It appeared that I'd suddenly run out of time.

Chapter 15

"Have you lost your mind?" I asked him. "You can't come here and point a gun at me. Someone's going to see you."

"Funny, they didn't notice me the last time I did it," he said. "Step aside."

I did as he ordered, and after he locked the door behind us, he cut straight to the chase. "Let me have it."

"Have what?" I asked.

"Don't play stupid with me. I saw Cora's journal when I was here before. I was about to break in when you showed up. I'm going to need that journal now."

"It's over there," I said, pointing to the counter. "Let me get it for you." The paperweight I'd just bought from Nancy was right there, and if I could use it to disarm Hicks, I'd pay Nancy the ten she'd first asked for it.

"Not so fast," he said. "I'll get it myself."

"What's wrong, Jimmy boy? Don't you trust me?"

"Don't call me that," he snapped as he moved toward the display case. I wish I'd hidden it better, but it didn't take him long to find the journal. "Surely that's not the reason you killed Cora and my cat," I said angrily.

"Watch yourself, Christy. If you make a move, you're dead."

I decided to do as he said, at least for the moment. He kept the journal on the counter and then started flipping through it. "Is this it? There has to be more."

"I don't know what you're talking about," I said.

"I don't believe you. She told me that she had proof, and she told me that if I didn't go to the police and confess, she'd turn over everything she had to them."

"When exactly did Cora confront you?" I asked.

"When do you think it was, genius?" Hicks snapped out, and I knew that Cora's threat had been the trigger that had set him off.

"Did it ever cross your simple little mind that she was just bluffing?" I asked, stunned by the revelation. "You most likely killed her for nothing. Why did you have to kill my cat, too?"

"He tried to protect her, if you can believe it. Oh, he died a hero's death, but he died just the same. That's why I'm wearing this bandage. If people saw it, they might suspect what had happened to me."

I was so proud of Midnight! He had died trying to save someone else, and that was my definition of hero no matter who did it. Could I do anything less? I wasn't about to stand there and be killed without putting up as much of a fight as my cat had. "I've never been more proud of him! I'm just sorry that he didn't get your eyes."

"He tried hard enough. I'm going to tell you what I wrote to Cora, Christy. This is your last chance."

"To sell you my shop? I won't do it."

"I know you won't. That's one of the reasons you're going to have to die, too. Cora wouldn't sell it to me, and when I wouldn't stop pushing her, she threatened to expose me. It's clear you won't sell the place to me, so I'll have to try my luck with Sandy and Mandy."

"What's so special about this place, anyway?" I asked.

"I've got a guy on the hook who wants to buy the block. You and Celeste are the last holdouts, and after I get my hands on this property, she'll cave, trust me on that. And if she doesn't, I'll just have to put a little heat on her, too. It's a pity you won't be around to see it, though. Now, do you know where she might hide something she didn't want anyone to find?"

My mind raced frantically for somewhere, and then I saw a movement in the doorway to the backroom. Midnight was there, and I could swear that he was summoning me with his neck. What did the rascal have in mind? I didn't have a clue, but I was willing to go along with him. "It might be in the backroom."

"Stay right here," he said. "If you move, I'll kill you."

"You'll never find it without me. Think about how many times you've tried to find it already," I said.

"Fine, but don't try anything. If you do, after I take care of you, I'll make sure that your roommate and your last cat pay the price. You don't want that, do you?"

I knew he was capable of what he was threatening, and it took my entire resolve not to plead with him to leave them alone. I was going to have to do this on my own though, with a little help from Midnight.

As I walked in the back, I searched for anything I could use as a weapon. I knew without much of a doubt that Cora's threat of more evidence was most likely empty. It was a real shame that she'd tried to bluff the wrong person.

Where could I lead him, though? Then I remembered the stack of boxes that were leaning precariously against the doorway. If I triggered them as I walked through, they might be heavy enough to dislodge the gun in Jim Hicks's hand.

As we approached the door, I could feel my heart pounding in my throat, and it seemed as though it was going to explode right in my chest. "Hit that light switch for me, would you?" I asked him.

As he reached for the switch, I kicked out at the boxes behind me.

It was beautiful the way they collapsed on my unsuspecting captor.

But the gun never left his hand, even though he hit the floor.

All I could do was run! I moved past him and started for the front door. I would have escaped out the back, but Emily had installed a double-keyed dead bolt lock instead of the single key I'd been used to. Opening it required a key from the inside as well as the outside, and I didn't have the time. I raced for the front, but I knew that I wasn't going to make it in time, and there was no doubt in my mind that Jim Hicks wouldn't hesitate shooting me in the back. I could feel his gun pointed straight at my spine, though I couldn't see him. My hand found the heavy paperweight as I reached the case, and as I picked it up, I turned toward him.

Throwing it with everything I had, it glanced off the side of his head, though I'd tried my best to break his nose with it. It did manage to stagger him.

I was running out of time, though.

I looked for something else heavy to throw, but all I could find was a barstool, and I knew that wouldn't stop him. Instead of aiming it at him, I hurled it through my front window.

The explosion was something to see as the stool landed on the sidewalk in a hail of glass hitting the concrete.

"Help!" I shouted with all my power, and then I leapt through the window and landed outside on my side. I had a pretty nasty cut on one elbow, and I hurt my shoulder with the impact. Pulling myself up, I looked for someone, anyone, to help me.

Imagine my delight when Sheriff Kent himself pulled his patrol car up in front of the shop and exited his car with his service revolver drawn.

"Jim Hicks is in there, and he's armed," I said frantically. For some reason, I added, "Don't let him shoot you!"

"Hold on," the sheriff said as he stepped up to the window. "Hicks," he shouted through the opening. "You've got three seconds to throw your weapon out, or I'm coming in."

I held my breath as I counted to myself, and I swore I got to five before the handgun clattered on the concrete a foot away from me. It appeared that he had no problem shooting me, but when it came to the possibility that someone might shoot back, he'd shown his true colors and chickened out.

After Hicks was safely handcuffed and in the back of the patrol car, Sheriff Kent came over to where I was sitting. I'd managed to nearly make it to a nearby bench, but then my legs finally gave out, and I barely made it there in time.

"Are you okay?" he asked as he sat down beside me.

I was holding a handkerchief against the cut on my arm.

"I think I sprained my shoulder."

"Throwing a chair through a window will do that to you," he said, his voice softer than I'd ever heard it.

"Actually, throwing was fine. It was the hard concrete landing that did it."

"You stay right here. I called an ambulance for you, and they'll be here any second."

"How did you know that I was in trouble?" I asked him. "Your timing couldn't be better."

"Actually, you owe that to your roommate. My niece called me right after the two of you spoke, and she was worried about you. She insisted that I check up on you."

"Did you arrest David Whitman?" I asked.

"Oh, yes. It appears that you had the misfortune of running into two of our worst citizens at the same time. It's amazing you came out of it relatively unscathed."

"In the scheme of things, I guess you could say that. I'm alive, at any rate." And so were Shadow and Marybeth. I might not have been able to save Cora and Midnight, but at least I'd managed to save them. That was what had made me so brave in the end. I didn't care so much about protecting my own life as I had my friends. I had to wonder about something, though. Now that the man who'd taken Midnight and Cora from me was going to get what he deserved, had I lost my ghost cat forever? As I looked back at the shop, I could swear that I saw Midnight's ghostly face appear in the opening that had up until recently been a window.

"Mrwerer," he said, and then vanished.

I smiled, but it died abruptly when I saw a puzzled look in Sheriff Kent's face.

"What's wrong?" I asked.

"I must be hearing things," he said.

"Why do you say that?"

"I could swear I just heard a cat. Did you hear anything?"

It would have been the perfect time to tell him about Midnight's reappearance into my life, but that was something

I wasn't in any mood to share with anyone else, at least not yet.

"It must have been the wind," I said, though the evening air was dead calm.

He accepted that, though. "Yeah, that must have been it."

I could swear I felt Midnight brush against me as I said it, but when I looked, he was nowhere to be seen.

After that, the trip to the hospital in the ambulance was almost uneventful.

My shoulder was just bruised, and the cut on my arm took all of four stitches. All in all, the sheriff was right. I'd had luck on my side tonight, but I'd also had something else a lot more powerful than that.

I'd had my Midnight, and even from the Great Beyond, he'd been there for me.

Our bond had reached beyond the abyss, and even though I knew that I would always miss the touch of his nose on my chin, and the full weight of him on my lap, in a way, he would be with me.

Made in the USA
San Bernardino, CA
23 August 2014